The Long-Timer Chronicles

TALES OF
TWO SISTERS

G. M. Lupo

Lupo Digital Services, LLC
Atlanta, GA

First edition (Pocket Paperback).

The material in this work was originally published in 2007
as *The Longtimers* (ISBN 1-4241-8826-1). It was subse-
quently republished as *The Long-Timer Chronicles: A
Tale of Two Sisters*, in 2011 (ISBN 978-0-9848913-0-6).

The graphic of the two sisters on the cover of this work
was created using an online AI generator, PlaygroundAI.
All other content, written or otherwise, is the original
work of the author.

ISNI: 0000 0005 0315 9196

ISBN: 978-0-9981595-7-7. Published by Lupo Digital
Services, LLC, Atlanta, Georgia (www.lupo.com). Printed
in the United States of America.

INTRODUCTION

The writing process which yielded my first published novel *The Longtimers* began in 2006 with my attempt to create a work using techniques I developed posting articles on the Internet. My process was to compose short, one-shot, humorous narratives that I edited quickly and posted immediately without overthinking them.

The first scene I committed to writing had been rolling around in my head for more than twenty years, since I first imagined it in college. A woman enters an art museum, and stops at a painting from hundreds of years before that resembles her. A man says, "Absolutely stunning." The woman thanks him, and when he turns to clarify he's talking about the painting, he realizes she looks like the woman in the painting. He excuses himself and the woman is joined by her husband who says, "Still turning heads, I see."

This couple became Charles and Renee Fox, and my plan was to center the story around them and their chief adversary, named Bergeron. Then, on the very first page, Bergeron murders a prostitute who shares the same attributes as him and the Foxes, and as I developed her story, she came to totally dominate the book. Her name was Vickie Seely, and she becomes Victoria Wells. At last, I understood a statement attributed to Tolstoy, about knowing his characters. The more I got to know Victoria, the less predictable she became. I'm happy for the opportunity to spend more time with her.

This represents my second attempt at resurrecting the storyline from The Longtimers. The first was a planned trilogy, and this one encompasses a planned four volumes. Reinventing involves rethinking, and taking the story in a new direction. Plus, my writing has evolved a great deal from the mid-aughts when I first worked on this piece.

I now present these tales to the reading public once again. It's hoped readers will find something worthwhile in these volumes. Enjoy!

OTHER WORK BY THE AUTHOR

G. M. Lupo is the author of these works:

- Worthy
- Atlanta Stories: Reconstruction
- Words Words Words: Essays, Poetry, Stories
- Rebecca Too
- Atlanta Stories: Fables of the New South

For new stories in development or to be added to the mailing list for future releases, visit the author's blog Raised by Wolves at http://gmlupo.com.

East
End

THE GARBAGE OF WHITECHAPEL

London, Whitechapel district, mid-November 1888, half past one in the morning.

Despite the cold and the furor over the Ripper killings, Vickie Seely makes her way along the dirty street, hoping for a client who will pay enough for her to afford the rent on a tiny flat she shares with two other women. She is poor, illiterate, and her family gave up on her years ago leaving her to fend for herself: begging; stealing; walking the streets, taking pence or shillings from smelly men who want a "quick one" before heading home to their families. She cannot recall the last time she had a complete meal, beyond some scraps a friendly pub owner passed to her as she was scavenging in an alley.

Prostitutes are common in this section of London, but Vickie doesn't look like the others. Her face and features are not marred by alcoholism or the hard living common to other residents of the area. She's shorter than average with a small frame, almost childlike. Her strawberry blond hair is pinned up and tucked beneath a weathered cap that's too big. As she walks, she hums a popular tune, stopping occasionally to correct a note or recall a lyric.

Ahead, she sees a well-dressed man heading her way. She falls into a slow saunter, staring in his direction and addresses him with a heavy Cockney accent.

"Ev'nin' sir. Lookin' for some comp'ny tonight?"

The man produces a gold sovereign bearing the likeness of the Queen.

"You are lonely. Vickie'll treat you right."

She leads him into an alley, but as she turns to prepare herself, he shoves her against the wall and wraps a cord around her neck, constricting her breathing. Desperate for air, she struggles to free herself, clawing at the rope to no avail.

"Not so fast, Vickie. I want to enjoy every minute."

Her body goes limp, and she slumps against the wall as she falls into darkness.

Manhattan, Upper West Side, early Fall, 2004, predawn.

A young, blonde woman named Dana, with a swimmer's physique, lies on her stomach on a king-sized bed that's messy from a night's sleep and perhaps a little more. She lifts her head and looks around then rolls over and sits up.

"Vickie? You here?"

Just outside the bedroom is an elegantly furnished living room. A baby grand piano sits in one corner with numerous paintings on the walls covering nearly every artistic genre of the twentieth century. Looking out of the window is a thin woman, smaller than average, with long, curly, strawberry blond hair, wearing a flannel housecoat. She idly, almost unconsciously, runs her fingers along an ugly scar across her throat.

She is Victoria Wells.

Without moving her eyes from the window, she turns her head slightly in the direction of the bedroom and speaks with a voice that still bears the faint traces of a cockney accent.

"It's okay, Sweetie. I'll be in straight away."

From the pocket of her housecoat, she produces a gold sovereign bearing the likeness of Queen Victoria and rolls it over the tops of her fingers. She steps away from the window, flips the coin into the air, catches it before it's halfway down, then heads into the bedroom.

When Margaret Smythe married Thomas Seely in Bishopsgate in 1834, she anticipated many years together and a houseful of healthy, happy children. When she learned she was pregnant, Margaret was certain the future was bright for her young family. Billy's birth made her happier than she had ever been. Margaret foresaw many years with Thomas raising their family.

Thomas was killed in an accident at the docks when Billy was barely two years old. Not long afterward, Margaret met Niles Gunnerson, a Norse seaman who answered an ad she placed for a lodger; Gunnerson paid on time and was quiet and kept his room tidy. One evening, she looked in on him just before bedtime and they allowed things to go much further. Their affair began in late September 1837 and concluded a couple of months later, when he shipped out for points unknown. A month later, Margaret discovered she was pregnant.

Margaret found herself unmarried and pregnant by a man who was no longer in the picture, a bad combination for early Victorian England. Her daughter with Gunnerson was born on Coronation day, 28 June 1838. Being a believer in signs, Margaret named the girl Victoria. Since Margaret had never married Gunnerson, Victoria could not have his name, so she became Victoria Seely. The local parish refused to baptize her, but kindly old Reverend Drake performed the ceremony in the church rectory after evening services had concluded.

Margaret soon discovered the severe stigma attached to women who had children out of wedlock. English law laid all the blame on the mother and no longer required the fathers to support the children, a moot point in Margaret's case since she didn't know how to find Gunnerson. She found it hard to get any work, even laundry and the neighbors who had been so kind to her when she was a young widow now shunned her and her "bastard" daughter.

She held up for as long as she could, but at last took to the bottle to relieve her misery. As resources became scarce, she resorted to the final indignity, taking men into her bed for money. Two years after Victoria was born, Margaret found she was pregnant again. This child, born late in 1840, she named Amanda, after her mother.

As Margaret continued her spiral into booze and prostitution, the children were neglected, and it frequently fell on kind-hearted neighbors to look after them. Education was out of the question, except for Billy who attended a local poor school sponsored by the church, where he was taught the basics of reading and writing and how to add and subtract and nothing more. The girls grew up ignorant and unloved, shunned by a society which vilified them. Billy did the best he could to look after his sisters, but there was only so much he could do as a young boy. As she got older, Victoria displayed a talent for music and was always humming or singing snippets of songs she'd heard around town.

When Victoria was eight, Niles Gunnerson returned. He explained to Margaret that he'd been traveling the world and that this was his first opportunity to get back to her. She stopped drinking, they resumed their physical relationship, and made plans to marry. Gunnerson was happy to learn of Victoria and to Margaret's delight, was willing to take responsibility for Amanda as well. On one of his visits, he gave Victoria a wooden flute which she learned to play quickly. Some neighborhood boys took it from her, prompting Billy to chase them down and beat them until they returned it with apologies.

It was the happiest Margaret had been since the time she had been with her husband, and for the first time, she tried being a mother to her daughters as well as her son. Then in March of 1848, a few weeks after Margaret learned she had another child on the way, Niles collapsed in the living room of Margaret's house and was pronounced dead by the doctor who arrived to tend to him.

Margaret's remaining months were spent preparing for the new baby by drinking a lot and lying in a near-cata-tonic state on the sofa in the living room. The events of the past few years kept swirling around in her head and the conclusion she finally came to was that her life had started to go wrong when Victoria was born. She made sure she shared this insight with Victoria whenever her daughter was nearby. By the time the new baby was due, Margaret had come up with a plan to rid herself of the causes of all her problems. She and Billy could start anew somewhere else.

Victoria welcomed the arrival of her little sister, named Sarah, a few months after her tenth birthday, but the joy was short-lived. Margaret announced about a month or so after Sarah came along that she'd given the baby to an "agency" which would take good care of her. In fact, she had paid Jackson and Hendricks, two malcontents she knew from the pub to help her dispose of the child. The following day, she marched Victoria and Amanda down to the local orphanage and left them on the steps with a note: "Do what you want with them. I don't care."

Margaret headed back to the house and went on a drinking binge to celebrate the start of her new life. Two days later, Billy found her dead on the floor of the kitchen. Because he was old enough and already a very strong boy, Billy was sent to a workhouse. It would be several years before he would see his sisters again.

Cedric Stepney and his wife Anne have always led exemplary lives. Cedric is a clothier, one of the "sons" of Stepney & Sons, a shop started by his father Everett some forty years ago. Cedric has retained the name even though his brother, Lemuel, the other "son" left to start his own haberdashery shop in Surry ten years past and Cedric has no children, let alone sons, to carry on the family business. He's a deacon at the local parish where Anne sings in the choir, and the Stepneys are known throughout their parish as the most generous and friendly people one could know, never too busy to lend a hand with a cause or to collect money for the poor.

A large, rotund, and jovial man with a booming bass voice, Cedric always plays Father Christmas in the local holiday pageant and Anne collects clothing or other donations, and often bakes up batches of cookies to give out to the children of the parish or to some wayward youth who happens across her doorstep. A woman of average height, but full-figured and shapely, Anne is the perfect complement to Cedric, with a slightly nervous demeanor that she covers with excessive cheerfulness. She dreams of the day she and Cedric will begin their family. Despite this, as each year slips by, they move closer to the time when it will be impossible to have children.

This afternoon they are making their way through the streets of Aldgate on their way home from the shop. For most of the twenty years they've been married, Anne has made it a habit to visit Cedric at his store then walk home with him. On this day, they take a slight detour as Anne spots a parcel of fabric she thinks would make good quilting material.

"Quite a bit of it, too," she says, as they approach the rolled-up fabric sitting on top of a stack of discarded boxes. Touching it, Anne looks at Cedric. "There's something in it."

She carefully removes the fabric but stops when she sees the top of a child's head. Cedric exclaims, "Oh God," as Anne removes the section covering its face.

The child's eyes are closed, its skin is pallid, its lips are blue, and it's not breathing. Anne cradles the baby in her arms as Cedric pulls back the remainder of the fabric.

"It's a little girl."

Anne sobs. "Oh, Cedric. Who could do something this horrible to someone so innocent?"

She presses her head to the baby's. "You poor little thing. You didn't have a chance."

"What should we do?"

"We can't leave her here. She deserves a proper burial." Anne's cheeks are soaked with tears, and she looks again at the tiny lifeless face then looks skyward. "Oh, God, why couldn't you have brought her to us? We'd have done right by her."

Suddenly, the baby's body starts trembling, frightening Anne who looks up at Cedric then back to the baby whose body convulses as she takes in a gasp of air. The Stepneys watch in amazement as the color returns to her face. Finally, she opens her eyes and begins moving in Anne's arms, seemingly no worse for the ordeal.

Wide-eyed, Anne stares, first at the baby then at Cedric.

"What's just happened, Cedric?"

"It's a miracle!" Cedric places his hand on the baby's head. "This is a sign from the Lord. He wants us to take this baby and raise her."

"Are you sure?"

"How else can you explain what we've just seen? Only the Lord can perform a miracle like that."

"I think you're right. But can we keep her? She must belong to somebody."

"Way I see it, anybody who'd dump her on a trash heap don't deserve her."

"You're right." Anne is indignant. "We should take her and raise her in a proper manner. This is a sign from the Lord."

Cedric taps his forehead with his right index finger. "Here, now, one of my clients is a judge with the Old Bailey. He's due for a fitting in a couple o' days. I'll sound him out on the best way to go about this. Make it all nice and legal. If he can't help us I grant you he'll know who can."

"That would be wonderful." She hugs the baby. "You rest easy little darling. We'll take good care of you."

As they walk toward their home, Cedric says, "What shall we name her?"

"What about Allison, after my mother?"

Cedric has another thought. "How about Allison Anne Stepney?"

Anne beams. "I like that."

Vickie's body lies in a heap in the alley, her eyes staring blankly into the darkness. Her face still wears the horrified look it bore during the attack. Finished strangling her, the attacker had removed the cord then took a knife from his coat pocket and drew it roughly across her throat, producing a steady trickle of blood, then shoved her onto the pavement.

He now stands, surveying his handiwork.

"Don't worry, dear. You didn't have much to look forward to anyway." He flips the sovereign toward her. "You earned it."

He moves toward the entrance of the alley but stops, contemplating something intently.

"Where to go, where to go. She'll probably be found around sunrise—"

He scans the street across from him until he sees a dark alcove set back from the street. "Just the place!"

He crosses the street and takes refuge in the alcove, leaning against the wall absent-mindedly whistling an indistinct tune and cleaning his fingernails with a pocketknife.

He springs to attention several minutes later when Vickie emerges from the alley, and he stares at her in a combination of amazement and confusion.

"It can't be."

He moves almost to the street as she heads away from him and tracks her until she has gone nearly a block then crosses, looking after her. He is seized by a sudden fit of laughter.

"After all these years, I've found you!"

He follows from a discrete distance.

On the second day the Seely sisters are at the orphanage, several older boys start harassing Amanda. Vickie rushes into the middle of them and grabs Amanda's hand, and they run toward the main living quarters where Miss Mary, the attendant, can usually be found. The boys chase them.

As they reach the door to the common area, Vickie pushes Amanda through. "Find Miss Mary."

She slams the door shut and tries to get away from the boys, but they catch her.

The one holding her says, "Time for some fun, eh?"

They drag her, screaming, into a laundry closet and bar the door behind them. After several minutes, she stops screaming.

Vickie walks with considerable difficulty toward the living quarters. Her clothes are dusty from the dirt on the floor of the laundry room and torn in several places. Her undergarments are bloody. Occasionally she stops to lean against the wall holding her stomach or to stifle a sob.

She enters the main room and Amanda calls out, "Vickie!" and rushes to her. "I couldn't find Miss Mary. The other girls said she's gone for the afternoon."

Vickie does not face her but looks away and continues walking with difficulty.

"What's wrong?" Amanda puts her arm around Vickie's waist and supports her. "What did they do?"

"Nothing. I'll be all right."

"Vickie, you've got to tell somebody. Miss Mary or Mr. Duggan."

"They won't believe me."

Amanda persists and the next day Vickie seeks out Mr. Duggan, the director, to tell him what happened. She finds him in a small office on the second floor of the orphanage.

"Victoria. What's wrong?"

Vickie starts to cry, and Duggan comes from behind his desk and guides her to a bench and sits beside her.

Before she can tell him about the incident, he runs his hand over her hair. "Have you any idea what a pretty thing you are?"

His abuse of her will continue for nearly four years.

Vickie occasionally sees Duggan eyeing Amanda and when she does, she asks to see him in his office. She isn't going to let him do to her sister what he's doing to her.

At last, the sisters escape to a life on the streets. Vickie never tells Billy about the abuse and swears Amanda to secrecy about it.

"If Billy finds out, he'll kill 'em all for sure. They'll send him to the gallows. I don't want that to happen."

Victoria is sitting on the bed, her head resting on Dana's shoulder.

"My brother says you're full of it."

"You told him?"

"A few days ago. He said no one lives that long."

"I said that myself once. But what did I know? There are quite a few of us. We're not wearing badges, so we're not easy to spot. I wouldn't have known about any of it if I hadn't met him."

"After what he did to you, why did you stay with him?"

"Bergeron can be very charming when he's not trying to slit your throat."

"Um, that's still a bit of a stretch."

"I don't know. Maybe, in a sick way, I looked at him as a father-figure."

"If that was my father, I'd have gone all Oedipus on him as soon as I got the chance. Though it probably wouldn't have worked in his case."

"Bergeron's entire attitude changed when he found out I was a long timer. He exposed me to art, music, and culture. He literally treated me like I was his daughter."

She sits up and leans her head on her fists.

"But no amount of good he did could ever make up for the fact that the first time he saw me, he lured me into an alley, strangled me, cut my throat then hung around to watch how people reacted when they found me."

They sit quietly for several minutes.

Dana moves so she's facing Victoria. "What were your actual parents like?"

"Barely knew my father." Victoria draws her knees up to her chest and rests her head on them. "Knew too much about my mother and most of what I knew I hated."

"I never knew my father or my mother."

"Aren't both your parents still alive?"

"The ones who raised me are."

"You're adopted?" Dana nods. "Why didn't I know this before now?"

Dana grins. "You have your secrets, I have mine. Don't get me wrong, if I'd had the opportunity to choose a set of parents, I'd have chosen the ones I have. But I still wonder about my birth parents. Who knows what's lurking in my medical history?"

"Do you have any chronic illnesses?"

"Never been sick a day in my life. No colds or flu, no chicken pox. George had it all."

"Have your parents told you anything about your birth mother?"

"She was sixteen, from Brooklyn, where they say I was born. She was an athlete — track, I think. They said she was very emotional when she gave me up but knew she couldn't take care of me."

Victoria sits up and rubs Dana's shoulder. "Maybe she's where you get your athletic abilities."

"Maybe. It must be nice not getting older."

"I age, just a lot slower. Something like one year for

every forty or fifty for average people."

"So, when I'm seventy, you'll be, twenty-five, twenty-six?"

"Somewhere in that neighborhood. For the first few years, I aged like everyone else then when I was eighteen, or so it slowed to a crawl." She lies back then rolls onto her side and props her head on her hand. "Not everyone has a traumatic experience like me. Most just figure it out when they outlive their friends and their children."

Dana rolls to her side. "You must lose a lot of people you care for over time. Ruth was the woman in the nursing home, right?"

"Yes. She was a chemical engineer. She took most of the photos of me from the forties to the seventies."

"How long were you together?"

"I met Ruth just after one of the worst days of my life, when Elizabeth Mayfair died in 1938 and I started to lose her in the mid-eighties."

"What happened?"

"Right at first, there were subtle signs: Confusion, forgetting dates or names, misplacing items. There was nothing I could do but watch as the woman I loved was torn apart, one memory at a time. When she couldn't be left alone, I found her a room in the best assisted living facility I could, and when they couldn't handle her any longer I had her transferred to the place near your gym."

"Would you visit me if I'm ever in that situation?"

"You better believe I would." Victoria leans in to kiss her. They snuggle for a few minutes then Victoria rolls onto her stomach, resting her head on her hands. "What exactly did you tell George?"

"That you've been alive since 1838 and watched them build the Empire State building. He doesn't believe a word of it."

"Did you tell him I have proof?"

"I did. He's going to bring his friend Rolf over, who specializes in appraising old photos. Aren't you afraid it might freak someone out when you tell them?"

"I'm open with you because we're intimate. I confide in my financial advisors and anyone who assists me with sensitive matters for obvious reasons. Most don't believe me or think I'm nuts. Those who believe me usually just say 'so what?' It's not like I have X-ray vision or can jump over buildings."

Victoria gets up from the bed. "You hungry?"

"Yes. Let me find some clothes. I'll join you."

"You don't have to get dressed for me."

Dana laughs.

"I don't like eating when I'm naked."

When Vickie enters her flat, her friend Alice is pacing and wringing her hands. She rushes over and clasps Vickie's shoulders.

"Where you been Vickie? I been worried sick." She sees blood on Vickie's dress. "Oh! What's all this?"

"It's blood. I think it's my blood."

"How can that be? You ain't got a scratch on you. What happened?"

"This man took me into an alley and choked me with a cord. When I woke up there was all this blood."

Alice points at her. "You met the Ripper, you did, and lived to talk about it. Dark Annie Chapman weren't so lucky."

Alice leads Vickie to one of the beds. "You lie down here. I'll see if we got something to help take the edge off."

"I just want to sleep. Try to forget about everything."

Vickie removes her outer garments but leaves on her slip and shoes.

"Bloody 'ell." Alice stares at a nasty scar on Vickie's neck.

"What?"

Alice pulls her over to the mirror. Vickie nearly faints when she sees the scar.

"Oh god. Do you think that's where the blood came from?"

"Can't be. That looks long healed over."

"But I didn't have it yesterday morning."

"I can't explain it then. Nobody heals up that fast."

"The sooner I get some sleep, the better. Maybe I'll wake up and find that this was all a bad dream."

"If it is, you and me is dreaming the same thing. You rest now, Vickie. I'll make certain nobody harms you."

In the morning, Vickie heads off to the park in hopes of seeing her brother Billy. She hasn't spoken to him in nearly twenty years — their last meeting had not ended well — but occasionally spies on him and his wife when they're in the park on Sunday to be certain he's healthy and happy.

She sets out at half past eleven and gets to the square within ten minutes. There, she's accosted by a man speaking in a thick Cockney accent who has a scarf wrapped around his neck, obscuring his face.

"Miss? Could I have a word?"

Vickie regards him with suspicion. "Do I know you?"

"We met once before, but it was a brief encounter."

"I ain't working now." She turns away.

"That's not what I meant." He steps in front of her to block her exit. "Please, ma'am, it's very important."

The wind blows the scarf away from his face and Vickie gets a good look and recognizes him.

"I know who you are. You're that man what tried to kill me last night. You're the Ripper!"

The man throws up his hands and leans toward her. "Please, don't be afraid. I'm not going to hurt you." He weighs this, tilting his head from side to side. "Any more than I already have."

"What you want then? Come to finish the job, did you?"

"No, I assure you, I just want to talk."

"Talk about what you done last night is it?"

"No. I'd rather talk about what happened after."

"What d'you mean?" Vickie eyes him suspiciously.

He leans closer to her. "I didn't try to kill you. When I left that alley, you weren't breathing, and your throat was cut. And then, just minutes later, you got up and walked away as though nothing happened."

Vickie moves away. "But something did happen, didn't it?"

"Yes, and I am truly sorry. I never would have touched

you if I had realized who you are."

"Who I am? I'm nobody, nothin'."

"You have no idea how special, how unique you are. But I can help you understand if you'll only let me."

"Why should I believe anything you say after last night?"

"You're right. You have no reason to trust me, and I don't blame you. But if you will give me a few minutes of your time, I can tell you incredible things about yourself. Things it will take you years to figure out on your own."

She seems to be considering what he's saying.

"If it will help to convince you, I have a very good cook and more food than you could eat in one sitting. You look like you could use a good meal."

"I ain't going nowhere with you alone, 'specially your house."

"We won't be alone. I have a full staff. If you say so, one or more of them can be present while we talk and can escort you from the house when we're done."

Vickie considers his proposal for a few seconds then looks at him sideways, narrowing one eye. "Have you got pastries?"

"I certainly do — and if there's nothing to your liking, my staff can get anything you want, anytime."

Vickie rubs her stomach. "I could do with a hot meal. But you try anything funny and I'm going to scream me head off, you got it?"

It has been eight years since Cedric and Anne found Allison. In the meantime, she has grown into a timid child, very intelligent, with a talent for drawing far beyond that of her peers. Aside from that her most distinctive feature is her hair, blonde with a reddish tint to it. Cedric built a small writing desk for her in the back room of the shop where she can sit and draw to her heart's content.

Today Cedric is at his shop looking after Allison who's out of school. As he's doing his regular inventory he hears a noise outside and he opens the rear door to find what he first mistakes for a grimy child picking through the garbage.

"Look here. What are you doing there?"

The person looks up at him and he realizes it's a small young woman.

"Please sir, I don't mean to bother you. I was only looking for some scraps to eat."

"Come closer, please. My eyes aren't what they used to be."

She approaches him and as he gets a better look at her face a glimmer of recognition hits him. It's as though he's looking into Allison's face as she might look in a few years and he imagines that this could have been her fate if her neglectful parents had kept her.

"What's your name young lady?"

"Vickie, sir."

"When did you last eat?"

"Can't rightly say, sir. Been a few days I reckon."

"Wait here."

Cedric returns to the back room. Allison looks up from her drawings. "Father, who's there?"

"Just someone in need of a hand."

Cedric goes to the cabinet and takes out the parcel containing his lunch. He takes it out to Vickie and gives it to her.

"Sir, you're being too generous. I can't accept all this."

"You have no choice, Vickie, because I'm not taking it back. Take it, enjoy it, and if you ever get the chance, do a good turn for someone else, all right?"

"I will sir." Vickie smiles and curtseys. "May God look kindly upon you."

Cedric glances in at Allison. "He already has Vickie."

When he goes back in, Allison is turned sideways at her desk watching him. "Father, why did you give that woman your lunch?"

"Missing one lunch isn't going to hurt me, but what I gave her might just save her life. You never go wrong by helping somebody. You remember that Allie."

Vickie stuffs the parcel she got from the shop owner under her coat and moves quickly through the alleys until she comes to a shed with a rickety door.

"Mandy?" She speaks in a loud whisper. "Mandy, you here?"

Her sister sticks her head out of the shed. "Right here."

Vickie joins her inside and sits on a box.

"Look what I got!"

Mandy sits beside her as Vickie opens the package the shop owner gave her. It's a loaf of bread, some dried meat, some fruit, and a bar of chocolate.

"Been quite a while since I seen that much food. Where'd you get it?"

"That place where the men buy their clothes, Stefanie's. The proprietor himself give it to me."

"I'm told he's a good man." She looks over the food. "Shouldn't we give thanks?"

"What we got to be thankful for? A few bites to keep us alive today so we can starve tomorrow?" Noting her sister's expression, Vickie relents. "Go ahead. Say whatever you want."

Mandy bows her head and mouths a prayer, concluding with, "Amen."

They dig into the food, making short work of it.

The sisters leave the shed and make their way through the alleys back toward Aldgate. A couple of young men from the docks start following them, making catcalls and whistles. Vickie and Mandy try to ignore them, but the men become more aggressive. Vickie catches Mandy's eye out of the corner of hers and gives a quick nod and they both start running.

The men chase them, howling and yipping like dogs. The girls manage to stay just ahead of them until they make a wrong turn and find themselves in a dead-end alley. The men corner them and advance, sneering at the girls.

"We're gonna have us a good time tonight, eh, Clive?"

"Right you are, Ollie."

Vickie pushes Mandy behind her. They back away from the men. She holds her hands in front of her.

Just as the men are right over them, a pair of powerful

hands grips each one by the collar of his shirt and slams their heads together then tosses them away from the girls. Vickie looks up into the face of her brother.

"Billy!"

She and Mandy jump up and hug him.

"Vickie. Mandy. I knew someone was in trouble, but I didn't realize who. I'm just thankful I got here in time."

"So are we," Mandy says.

"Come on. I got a room for the rest of the week. It's not very big, but you can have the bed and I'll take the floor."

When Vickie and the man arrive at his residence, they are greeted by a chubby, brown-haired man wearing a dark waistcoat, who addresses the man as "Mr. Bergeron".

The servant looks Vickie over and rolls his eyes.

"Giles, this is Vickie. She'll be dining with us this evening and may stay on as our guest if I can convince her."

"Pleased to make your acquaintance, Mr. Giles." Vickie gives a slight curtsey.

"Just Giles, ma'am." He has a vaguely noticeable scowl on his face. "I'll inform cook, sir."

"Tell her to put together a tray of pastries for our guest and a pot of tea. We'll be in the study."

"Very good sir." Giles bows then disappears down a hallway.

"This way. My study is on the third floor. We can talk there in private."

"Private?" Vickie has a note of fear in her voice.

"Just talk, remember?"

As they ascend the steps, Bergeron says, "Vickie? Is that short for Victoria?"

"Yes sir. Me mum named me for the Queen."

On the way up, they encounter a matronly woman who appears to be in her thirties. She cheerfully greets Bergeron as she passes him then nods to Vickie.

"Mrs. Mayfair. This is Victoria. I need you to prepare the guest room in case she decides to stay with us. Also round up some clean clothes for her."

"Certainly, sir." She examines Vickie. "My, you're a tiny thing. Still, I think I can find something."

"Thank you, ma'am."

In the study, Bergeron directs Vickie to a large leather chair, and he sits in a similar one across from her.

"First, let me introduce myself. As you may have surmised, I'm known as Bergeron, a man of independent means, a world traveler—"

"The Ripper."

"Do not bring that up again." Bergeron places his hand over his eyes. "I deeply regret what happened. What I'm about to tell you should help to make up for it."

He leans back in the chair then takes a cigar from a nearby case and lights it.

"Enough about me. Tell me about you. Where are you from? What's your family like?"

She speaks as though reciting from a script she read but only barely memorized. "I'm Vickie Seely. Me mum told me I was born in Bishopsgate. Met me dad when I was eight or nine, but never got to know him very well. They're both dead now."

"Do you have any idea when you were born?"

"Oh, I know exactly when I was born." Vickie speaks with pride. "Me mum told me — Coronation day."

"Coronation day?"

"When Queen Victoria took the throne. That's why Mum called me Victoria, after the Queen."

Bergeron considers it a moment and chuckles. "Coronation day." He rises and goes to the mirror then motions to her. "Join me over here."

Vickie hesitates then rises and moves cautiously to where he is. He places his hands gently on her shoulders and guides her so she's directly in front of the mirror.

"I want you to take a good long look at yourself." Vickie does as she's told. "And I will tell you that Coronation day was fifty years ago."

Vickie gasps. Her implied age does not match the youthful reflection that confronts her in the mirror.

"That long. Me friends used to kid about how I never seemed to get any older. I always thought I was just one of the lucky ones what don't show their ages."

"Oh, you are one of the lucky ones — more so than you can ever imagine. You see, my dear, you are going to look this way for hundreds of years."

Vickie pulls away and looks at him with a confused expression.

"Are you mad? Nobody lives that long."

Bergeron chuckles then puts his arm around her shoulders and draws her back to the mirror.

"We do."

There's a tap on the door then Giles enters with a tray containing a teapot, some cups, saucers and dessert plates, a sugar bowl and creamer and a plate piled high with a variety of pastries.

"Your pastries, ma'am."

"Thank you, Mr. Giles."

"Just Giles, ma'am." He speaks with the slightest hint of annoyance in his voice.

Bergeron detects the tone. "Giles, let me make something very clear to you. While she is in this house, Victoria is to be treated as you treat me. No less. Do you understand?"

"Yes sir. Sorry sir, ma'am."

He waits a moment, until Bergeron relents. "That will be all for now, Giles. Inform cook we'll be dining around eight."

"Yes sir." Giles bows, then leaves.

Bergeron looks back to Vickie to see her giving him an anxious look.

"Go ahead. They're all for you if you want them."

"Thank you, sir." She practically swallows one whole while piling several more on a plate then pours a cup of tea, adding cream and several cubes of sugar and takes the pastries and cup back to the leather chair. She gobbles up each pastry as fast as she can shove it into her mouth.

"Now, Miss Seely, while you're enjoying your food, let me give you some background on who we are."

"What d'you mean we?" She speaks between chews, her mouth almost full.

He mulls this over for a moment. "I'm not certain there is a formal name for what we are. Those I've encountered refer to themselves as long timers." He looks at her shoving another pastry into her mouth. "Pause a moment as soon as you've swallowed what's in your mouth, I want to ask you something."

It takes her several minutes to chew all she has in her mouth, but finally she swallows it. "What d'you want to ask me?"

"In your opinion, what's an average lifespan?"

"Lifespan?"

"I mean, how long does the average person live?"

"Oh." She considers it. "Where I come from, you're lucky if you make it past forty or fifty."

"Right." She gives him a questioning look and he waves his hand toward her. "You may continue."

She starts eating again.

"Your situation is unique as you've endured a traumatic experience."

She starts to speak up, but he raises his hand. "I know, I know."

She continues eating.

"I also endured such an experience. My family was slaughtered, and I was the only survivor even though I was attacked as well. By this time, I had already begun to notice differences in myself and those around me."

"What kind of differences?"

"I was in my forties when my family was killed but looked much younger than my colleagues with whom I served in the army. When I was in my twenties, there was a nasty fever that killed my brother plus many of my brothers in arms and even though I was exposed to people who were sick and the same conditions as those who had it I never came down with it. I tended to recover quicker than my colleagues after long marches or harsh combat. You yourself said that your contemporaries had noted that you didn't seem to get any older. I suspect you were only a few years away from realizing you lived longer as well."

Vickie nods then goes and refills her plate and cup. She

holds up a pastry and gestures with it. "How many of us are there?"

"Hard to say. We look and act like everyone else. One way to tell is if you get to age forty or fifty but still look like you're in your twenties. Another is if you are killed by some unnatural means and return from the dead. There are other ways, but they're somewhat unpleasant."

"Like what?"

"Put your plate down and come over here." He reaches into his pocket as she does as he instructs. "Let me see your hand."

She holds out her right hand and Bergeron takes it and examines it a moment then suddenly pulls a knife out of his pocket and slices her hand.

She screams and pulls away from him. "What the bloody 'ell are you doing?"

"Don't cover it. Hold your hand out and watch."

Reluctantly, she does as he says. Bergeron drops the knife onto his desk and joins her then takes her hand, holding it up where she can see the cut. As she watches, the cut heals itself in a matter of minutes. Bergeron releases her hand, but she holds it there, staring wide-eyed at it.

"It's true. All you been saying is true, ain't it?"

Bergeron leans on his desk. "Yes. That's why you're still walking around after last night, why you're going to continue to walk around for a thousand or more years."

"Is that possible?"

"I was born during the reign of Caesar Augustus, over nineteen hundred years ago."

She eyes him suspiciously. "You look really good for your age."

"Thank you."

Vickie paces away from him then turns back, pointing at him. "Okay, I believe what you're telling me. And I'll agree I could probably learn a bit from you." She walks to him and puts her hands on her hips. "But I ain't agreeing to nothing until I get an explanation for last night."

She marches back to her chair, retrieves her pastries and sits.

Bergeron stares at her a moment then sits across from her. "Have you ever killed anyone, Vickie?"

"Matter of fact, I have. But he hurt someone I cared a lot about." She leans forward. "What did I do to deserve what I got from you?"

He leans back and looks away from her. "The simple answer is you were there. I set out last night looking for someone and there you were."

"So, you're saying that if somebody else came along, you'd have gotten them."

"Not necessarily. A long time ago I devised a test in order to identify someone like myself. No one ever passed before you." He pauses and reflects on the statement. "Well, there was one other, but I try not to think about her anymore."

Bergeron stands and walks to the window. "It's been centuries since I've had to think about my motivations." He gazes out the window. "I was born a proud Roman. Blood and gore wasn't just a fact of life, it was a means of entertainment. Two men fought a pitched battle, sometimes for hours and the fate of one or both rested on the whim of a single man. I was also in the army and the Roman method of battle was man to man in close quarters. I lost count of the men whose lives I ended with the point of my sword, usually while staring them right in the eye."

He paces anxiously in front of Vickie, his right hand smoothing back his hair. "Okay, look, if you want a detailed explanation for what happened last night, I don't have one. You were there. I was there. The moment seemed right. What can I say?"

Vickie stands and confronts him. "Don't say nothing. Just listen. I know you want me to stay here, and I think I know why. First, I want to know what you expect in return."

"Your company. It's not often I run across someone I know will be around the length of time I will. I'd like to talk, to share my insights about life and to help you along the way."

"All right, then. If you want me to stay then what happened last night can't happen again. And I'm not just talking about me, I'm talking about anybody. No more of that, you got it?"

Bergeron shrugs. "A small price to pay."

Vickie nods. "All right then, let's shake on it."

They shake hands.

Bergeron motions toward her chair. "Sit down and let me ask you something. If you could pick one thing you've always wanted to do, what would that be?"

"Oh, that's easy, play piano."

"Piano?"

"I always had a head for music, and I always loved hearing piano music. Plus, I got long fingers. Somebody told me that would make it easy for me to play."

"Very well." Bergeron goes to the door and calls for Mrs. Mayfair.

"Yes sir?" Mrs. Mayfair says when she appears in the room.

"I believe I've convinced Victoria to stay with us, and she's just informed me she's always wanted to learn to play the piano. You have a friend who gives lessons don't you?"

"Yes sir, my cousin's wife."

"Ask her to stop by sometime tomorrow to make arrangements, and also have someone tune the piano in the front parlor."

"I will sir. Pleased to hear you'll be sticking around."

Once Mrs. Mayfair leaves, Bergeron continues. "Tonight, when you retire to your quarters, make a list of what you want to accomplish. Write it all down and we'll start working on it."

Vickie frowns. "Well, to be honest, the first item would probably be to learn to read and write."

Bergeron nods. "So be it. Anything else, tell Mrs. Mayfair."

Vickie hurries through the streets, desperate to make it to the jail before the court has convened. She's trying to free her sister, who's been caught picking pockets, the fourth time over the past several months that she's been pinched for the crime. Vickie has managed to raise enough money to hopefully get her paroled. As soon as she arrives, however, she realizes she's too late. Mandy and several others are being led out in irons to waiting carriages.

"Mandy! Mandy, what's happened?"

"They've sentenced me. I'm being sent down to Australia. We're to be on our way this evening."

"No! They can't do that. Isn't there something we can do?"

"Vickie, it's okay. It's a new country. Maybe I can get down there and make something of myself after all."

"What am I going to do without you? You've been my rock all these years."

"No, you've been mine. You'll be fine and so will I."

Vickie throws her arms around Mandy then kisses her several times on each cheek. Vickie holds her until one of the guards pulls Mandy away.

"Once you get settled contact us. Send it to Billy's. Let us know how you're doing."

"I will."

She's loaded into a carriage and as they start to pull away she yells to Vickie.

"Maybe you'll make it down there someday yourself."

Vickie looks after them, waving until the carriage is completely out of sight.

Dana lets her brother George and his friend Rolf into the apartment. George is medium height with dark hair and wears glasses with black plastic frames. Rolf, a stout man with reddish hair and a neatly trimmed beard, stops to admire the many paintings on the wall.

"What the—" His eyes fall on a Cubist painting. "This is a very good imitation of Picasso's style."

Dana gives him a smile. "It's by Picasso. Look at the inscription."

Rolf gives her a skeptical look then leans in. "Para Victoria." He shakes his head. "I've studied Picasso's work for a number of years, and I've never seen this one before."

"Vickie can give you the full story." Dana indicates the paintings. "But every painting on this wall is an original."

Rolf scans the collection, visably impressed.

"Then it's worth a fortune: Monet, Van Gogh, Juan Gris, Klee, Derain, Warhol. This is one of the best private collections I've ever seen in one place."

George gestures impatiently. "Where is she?"

"In the bedroom." Dana guides them to the dining area. "She didn't want to color your judgment one way or another."

Several chairs have been pulled around one end of the dining room table and the rest arranged against the wall in regular intervals. Rolf moves to the end of the table.

"Yes. I've never been asked to authenticate a person before, so I'm not sure what the precedent is."

He sets a large case onto the table and opens it, removing a few items such as a magnifying glass and a jeweler's eyepiece.

George lets out an exasperated sigh. "You're just going to look at some old pictures and tell us if they're authentic."

"The pictures I can handle. Give me a couple of minutes to set up and we can get started."

Dana goes to a shelf and retrieves several scrapbooks filled with photographs and takes them to where Rolf is sitting. She sets the oldest looking one in front of him. "Start with this."

He thumbs through the pages, giving each one a cursory examination. Occasionally he stops at a photo and takes a closer look. In one instance, he says, "Scott Joplin?" He examines them closely with a magnifying glass and the jeweler's eyepiece. Then he places a few on the light box and looks them over again.

Rolf opens the picture folder and the first thing his eyes fall on is a sepia toned photo of a woman with light-colored curly hair, dressed in a low-cut party gown in a style like the late-nineteenth century. He sets it to the side then takes out a black and white shot of the same woman wearing modest Depression-era clothing, standing across the street from a building in its earliest stages of construction. The street signs are visible above her head, 34th Street and 5th Avenue.

"The Empire State Building." Rolf shows the photo to George. "Or should I say the Empire State Really Big Hole."

Rolf takes the oldest of the pictures, the sepia-toned turn-of-the-century shot and closely examines the edges and back. "Gautier. This looks like their work."

He glances at George and Dana standing nearby.

"The paper's right and the composition looks like what they were doing in the 1890s to 1900s."

He scans it with the magnifying glass. "The signs of age look genuine as well." Looking back to the image, the next thing to catch his eye is the noticeable scar along the woman's throat.

He spends several minutes examining the photo with the jeweler's eyepiece and magnifying glass then places it onto the light panel. He examines it a while longer using various other tools. "In my judgment, and without more extensive lab tests or a chemical analysis of the paper or photographic materials, I'd have to say this photo is genuine."

He holds up the sepia-toned photo. "This is not a composite of two shots and the signs of wear actually traverse the image. That's hard to fake." Rolf turns the photo over. "It says on back it was made at Gautier studios. That was a major photography shop in Paris from around 1885 through the early twenties. I've seen lots of photos made at Gautier and this is a textbook example of their work from that period." He holds up the photo and points to it. "The scenic backdrop behind her was one of their more popular backgrounds. It's been in more photos than I can count."

"Told you so." Dana whacks George in the arm.

"We're not quite finished yet." Rolf sets the photo aside.

He subjects several other photos which appear to be from the turn of the century through the 1950s to the same examination as the first photo. Finally, he places the last photo back into the folder. "In my professional judgment, these are also genuine photos from the period they appear to represent."

George leans over the table. "Are you absolutely sure?"

Rolf shrugs.

"No one can be absolutely sure, but I will say this, if these are fakes, they're damn good fakes. I can't find a single discrepancy with any of them. The paper's right, they have the appropriate signs of aging and there's no obvious photo manipulation or other signs of tampering. The grain, the shading, everything looks genuine."

Dana bounces up and down clapping. "Vickie will be so happy!"

George shakes his head. "Go get her."

Dana disappears into the bedroom and a minute or so later, she emerges, followed by a woman with long, strawberry blond hair, wearing jeans and a gray Henley shirt. She's wearing a red scarf around her neck and her hair is pulled back into a loose French braid. "Rolf and George, Victoria Wells."

Rolf rises and walks toward her, staring intently. "Unbelievable."

He stops a few feet away from her then shakes his head and laughs. "Ms. Wells, I must say you do look an awful lot like your — grandmother, great-grandmother?"

Victoria smiles. "I thought you'd say something like that. But would a great-granddaughter have this?" She pulls the scarf away, exposing the scar. Rolf's eyes widen and he moves closer, staring at it.

"My god." He leans in and reaches toward her neck but stops before he touches her skin. He meets her eyes. "May I?" Victoria nods. He runs his finger along part of the scar then straightens. "Come over here".

They head back to where the folder is.

Victoria stands before him as he looks, first from the oldest photo then back to her.

George throws up his hands. "Maybe she cut herself to look like the picture."

"You can't fake this." Rolf indicates the scar. "It looked nasty in the photo, but seeing it closer, I wonder how you survived the cut."

Victoria pulls out a chair and sits down. "I didn't. I was strangled first. The cut came after my heart stopped. I believe it was intended as some sort of test. I'm told I was the first person to pass."

Rolf is very interested. "Where'd it happen?"

"Whitechapel, November of 1888."

This catches George's attention. "Jack the Ripper attacked you?"

"Attacked and killed me. My body can heal itself quicker than an average person. It's the same for all of us."

"All of you?" Rolf says.

"I'm not the only one with a long lifespan. I've met several others and I'm sure there are more. In some circles they refer to themselves as 'long-timers'."

George holds up his hand. "Wait a minute. Weren't all of the Ripper's victims—"

Victoria stops him. "Yes. And in answer to your next question, yes, I was. I'm not especially proud of how I lived my life back then. I figured I'd just die of consumption or cholera or some other ailment if I wasn't murdered first, so what difference did it make. Then I learned I had all the time in the world to do whatever I wanted. It gave me a whole new perspective on life."

She rises.

"If we're finished here, let's go into the living room. I've got some snacks in the kitchen, and you can help yourselves to the bar."

Rolf makes a beeline for the Cubist painting.

"I've studied Picasso's work for nearly twenty years. Why don't I know this painting if it's by him?"

"Because no one's ever seen it. Pablo painted it just for me while I was living in Paris as repayment of a loan."

"You knew Picasso?" George says.

"Starting to believe me are you? Yes, I knew Picasso, Braque, Guillaume Apollinaire, Gertrude and Alice. Stayed at their place a few times, in fact. I knew Hemingway and Fitzgerald. In fact, it was Scott who convinced me to come back to New York. Not personally, but through his writing. So, I came back, bought this place and I've been here ever since."

THE GARBAGE OF WHITECHAPEL

"You've lived here that long?" Rolf says.

"I have." Victoria goes to the shelves in the dining room and picks up another folder. She sits on the couch and places the folder on the coffee table. Dana sits beside her and leans against her. "Here's my original deed." Victoria produces a yellowing piece of paper. "Here's the one we drew up when I 'inherited' the place from my namesake Aunt Victoria. And here's another."

Rolf takes the papers and holds them together to compare the signatures. He looks at George. "You're the handwriting expert, you should look these over."

George steps into the dining room and grabs the magnifying glass and jeweler's eyepiece. He sits and places the documents on a tray beside him and looks over the signatures from the various periods.

"Yes, I would have to say these do appear to have been done by the same person." He stands and hands the documents back to Victoria. "So, it seems that we are in the presence of a one hundred and sixty-six-year-old woman. And you don't look a day over twenty-five."

Dana puts her arm around Victoria's shoulder and gives her a squeeze. "Told you so."

Around seven, Bergeron checks his watch.

"We'll be dining in an hour. You should get washed up and try on some clean clothes."

He goes to the door, where Giles is standing outside.

"Send Mrs. Mayfair up."

A few minutes later, Mrs. Mayfair enters and presents herself to Bergeron.

"Have you had any luck in rounding up clothes for Victoria?"

"I have, sir. It's kind of a mixed batch, but they'll do until we can get her some proper clothing."

"Very good. Show her to the guest room and draw a bath for her."

Mrs. Mayfair nods and goes over to Vickie. "Well, now, Miss, let's see what we can do for you."

Vickie follows her down the stairs.

"How long have you been with Mr. Bergeron?"

"'Bout ten years now. I came to work for him right after I lost my husband, Wilton."

As they reach the landing, Vickie says, "Have you noticed anything peculiar about him? About how he looks, that is."

Mrs. Mayfair stops, leans toward Vickie, and speaks confidentially. "Are you asking me if I've noticed he doesn't seem to be getting any older?"

Vickie blushes. "Yeah, that's what I was gettin' at."

"Most of the oldest servants know. We figured it out after being here a few years. The staff that rotates in and out never find out."

Vickie nods. "Then maybe you should also know—"

"That you're like him?"

"How'd you know that?"

Mrs. Mayfair starts walking again but continues in a loud whisper. "It's not every day he brings home a young lady. In fact, before you, it was never. He seems to be taking an interest in you and the only reason I can think of is that you're like him."

"I guess that makes sense."

"So how old are you?"

"Mr. Bergeron says I'm fifty."

Mrs. Mayfair shakes her head. "You would have to be older than I am. You look like you could be my daughter if I had one."

Mrs. Mayfair shows Vickie into the guest room. "You get out of those clothes and try on some of those over there. They should do for this evening and tomorrow we can go out and get you a whole new wardrobe." She examines Vickie's feet. "How long's it been since you had those shoes off?"

"Couple o' days ma'am. I slept in 'em last night."

"You slept in your shoes?"

"Had to, ma'am. Where I come from, if you don't, you wake up and they're gone. Sometimes you still wake up and they're gone along with your feet."

"You don't ever have to worry about that again." Mrs. Mayfair shakes her finger at Vickie. "Now I'm going to get you some fresh towels. You get ready for your bath."

"Thank you, ma'am." Vickie curtsies. "I appreciate all you're doing for me."

Mrs. Mayfair leaves. Vickie takes a moment to look around the room then sits on the bed and bounces a time or two. She unlaces her shoes then pulls them off. When she removes her right shoe something heavy drops onto the floor. Vickie bends down and picks it up. It's the gold sovereign Bergeron offered her which she jammed into her shoe after finding it when she woke up in the alley. She holds it up to the light.

"You may just be my lucky coin after all."

EXTREME MAKEOVER: LONDON EDITION

After a bath and a good night's sleep, Vickie awakens to a knock at her door. She looks up from under the covers to be greeted by Mrs. Mayfair.

"Cook's put on a nice hot breakfast for you. If you're ready I can bring it up and we can talk about what we're going to do today."

"That would be nice."

Mrs. Mayfair goes to get breakfast and Vickie gets up and puts on her robe and slippers. When Mrs. Mayfair returns, Vickie is seated at a small table facing away from the door. Mrs. Mayfair places the tray on the table and looks at Vickie. The first thing she sees is the scar.

She gasps. "Oh my."

"What?" Vickie remembers and touches her neck. "Oh yeah, I keep forgetting about this."

"How could you forget?"

"I didn't have it two days ago."

"Two days?" She motions that she'd like to take a closer look and Vickie nods. Mrs. Mayfair runs her fingers lightly over the scar. "Where'd you get it if you don't mind me asking?"

Vickie looks away from her.

"I think for both our sakes, it'd be best if I don't answer."

Mrs. Mayfair looks at her then up in the direction of Bergeron's study. "Say no more. But if that's so then why—"

Vickie shrugs. "You may find this 'ard to believe, but it's better than where I come from."

Mrs. Mayfair pats Vickie's hand. "Well don't you worry, dear. Liz Mayfair will keep a close watch over you."

"Thank you. And Vickie Seely will do 'er best to look out for you too."

Vickie leans over the plate and begins shoveling food into her mouth with the spoon. Mrs. Mayfair gives her a disgusted look and slaps her hand.

"Here, now. That's no way for a proper lady to eat."

"What d'you mean?"

Mrs. Mayfair takes the silverware and holds it in the proper manner for dining.

"Like this." She mimics eating. "Here, you try."

She hands the knife and fork back.

Vickie looks at her with uncertainty then tries holding the utensils in the manner Mrs. Mayfair has shown. She takes a few bites.

"That's better. You'll pick it up."

Vickie nods.

"So, you going to follow me around to make sure I do everything right?"

"There'll be some of that I suppose. But I'll mainly guide you in the household items then your other teachers can do the rest."

Victoria enters the ground floor of the Montgomery Trust building in Manhattan the first day of Fall 1911, and walks to the reception counter. Behind it, a harried young man is trying to field calls and direct visitors.

"Excuse me."

The man looks at her. "If you're here for a secretarial position the hiring office is down the hall and to the right."

"But I'm—"

"Down the hall to the right." The man points in the direction she should go then turns his attention to a quartet of men at the opposite end of the counter.

Victoria wanders away from the counter then goes to look at the directory, hoping for some idea of where she should go.

A man's voice comes from beside her. "Excuse me, Miss?"

She turns to find a man of medium height, with short-cropped red hair, wearing wire-framed glasses and holding a briefcase. "Can I help you find something?"

"Yes. I have some money I'd like to invest."

"Do you mean as a sort of Christmas fund?"

"No, long term."

"Very good." He extends his hand. "I'm Stanley Reed and I can assist you."

"Thank-you Mr. Reed. I'm Victoria Wells."

Reed directs her to his desk.

"Is this for you and your husband?"

"I'm not married. I work in the music business and have met with some success."

"What do you do?"

"I'm a pianist, and I write music."

"Really? Have you written anything I'd have heard?"

"Have you heard Starlight and Memories?"

Reed stops. "Victoria. You're V. Wells!"

"That's me."

"My wife has been teaching that to our son and daughter lately. I've probably heard it a hundred times but never seem to get tired of it."

They reach his desk and are seated.

"I don't know if that's a testament to my writing ability or to their playing. But thanks for the compliment."

"There's just something in the melody I find pleasing." He removes some forms from his desk. "Now, how much are you looking to invest?"

"I'm consolidating several accounts. I've recently been transferring my remaining assets from England, and I don't want to stash them in some account that's going to just sit there."

"I thought I detected a bit of an accent. How long have you been in America?"

"Not quite ten years. We came here in 1902."

"You must have come with your parents then. I can't imagine you were very old when you made the crossing."

"That's something we'll need to discuss. For now, I'd like to start with two hundred and forty thousand dollars."

Several of the other accountants turn their heads when they hear the amount.

"That's quite a nest egg."

"Is that going to present a problem?"

"Oh no," Reed says. "We are well-equipped to handle a deposit of that size." He starts to fill out the paperwork then says, "Why don't we get all your assets here first then I can begin to advise you on prudent ways to make the most of them."

"Wonderful."

Several weeks later, Victoria is in the conference room waiting for Stanley Reed. He enters with a file folder and sits across from her.

"Now, Miss Wells, I have confirmed that all your funds have cleared and we're ready to do business."

"Wonderful news, Mr. Reed. But first, there's something you need to know."

"Yes?"

"Understand that I don't expect you to believe what I'm about to tell you. And that's why I wanted to wait until the money was all here so you wouldn't think I'm a crackpot." She touches his hand. "I also must ask that you not reveal what I'm about to say to anyone. Not your boss, not even your wife."

He responds with a nervous chuckle. "I have no problem keeping your personal details private."

"Good."

She removes from her purse a photo of her with Mrs. Mayfair when they came to America.

"You asked how old I was when we immigrated. This is a photo I took with Elizabeth, my friend and assistant, a few days after we got here."

Reed takes it and looks from it to Victoria.

"You haven't changed much."

"I haven't changed at all." She hands him another photo "This is another of me and Elizabeth taken a few weeks ago."

Reed notes that while Elizabeth has obviously aged that Victoria looks pretty much the same.

She removes one final photo and slides it across the desk to him. "This was taken in Paris in 1893."

"1893?" Reed says as he looks at the sepia-toned photo of Victoria in her party dress. "This can't be you."

Victoria checks to be sure no one is around. She unbuttons a few buttons on her blouse. "I assure you it is."

She opens her collar to show him her neck. Reed's eyes

widen and he looks once again between the photo and Victoria. She buttons her blouse.

"How is this possible?"

Victoria explains what she knows about herself and her lifespan. Reed listens with a disbelieving look on his face.

"This is incredible. I'll be honest and say that I find much of it very hard to believe."

"You don't have to believe it. In time you'll know I'm telling the truth. Right now, all I need you to do is advise me in my finances as best as you can."

"That I am equipped to do."

"And we can afford to be a bit aggressive. I have a very long time until I'll need to worry about retirement."

Allison, thirteen, is walking toward her father's shop, her drawing pad under her arm. She's been at the park sketching scenes most of the afternoon. Half a block from Stepney & Sons, a policeman overtakes her and grabs her roughly by the arm.

"Looking for some fresh pockets eh, Vickie?"

"Let me go. I don't know any Vickie."

"We'll talk about that down at the precinct." The officer starts to pull Allison along with him. She breaks away and rushes toward her father's shop with the policeman in hot pursuit, blowing a whistle.

Allison runs into Stepney & Sons. "Father! Father!"

Cedric enters just as the policeman comes through the front door. The officer grabs Allison by the arm causing her to drop her pad. "Thought you'd get away, eh, Vickie?"

He raises his hand to strike her but Cedric steps from behind the counter, and puts his arm in front of Allison.

"Don't you dare lay a hand on my daughter!"

The policeman releases Allison, who runs behind the counter.

"Daughter? Mr. Stepney, I didn't realize she was your daughter."

"She most certainly is, and even if she wasn't, there's no reason to raise your hand to her. You're twice her size."

He looks back at Allison cowering behind the counter. "You've got her scared out of her wits. What's the meaning of this?"

"Sorry sir." He removes his hat. "But she looks like a known pickpocket said to inhabit these neighborhoods."

"I assure you, officer, my Allie hasn't picked anyone's pocket. She's a decent and hardworking girl and attends church every week with her mother and me. When she's not at school, she's usually helping here and rarely out of our sight otherwise."

"I apologize, sir." The officer bows his head.

Cedric motions for Allison to come forward.

"It's not me you owe an apology."

The patrolman stoops down and picks up Allison's drawing pad and hands it to her. "Miss Stepney, I deeply regret this mistake on my part. It will never happen again."

Allison gives him a cold stare as she receives the pad. "No harm done."

Cedric runs his hand over the back of her head. "You see, officer. She's as forgiving as anyone could be." He hands a writing pad to the officer. "I, however, am not certain I'm satisfied. Write your name and your superior's name. I'll decide what to do with the information once I've had more time to reflect on this incident."

"Yes sir." The officer writes.

"Allie, you go in back and relax. We'll make sure this doesn't happen anymore."

"Thank you, Father." She exits behind the curtain.

"This pickpocket, what's her name?"

"We know her as Vickie. She mainly works around the theater district, but she's been sited 'round Whitechapel and Aldgate as well."

"Next time, be more inquisitive. Allison is well-known in this neighborhood."

"Yes sir." He dons his cap and leaves.

Cedric looks after him.

"Vickie? Why is that name familiar to me?"

Early in 1984, Victoria decides to get more involved in the charity she started in the sixties, Caring Hands, Loving Hearts. One of the projects they fund is a shelter and halfway house for women fleeing the streets or from abusive relationships. One of the first orders of business is to find a new director. Victoria plows through stacks of people with impressive resumes and much experience, but her eyes settle on one applicant, named Wanda Jefferies, and Victoria makes a note to interview her at the earliest opportunity.

Wanda is a large, shapely Black woman in her late thirties. She wears her emotions on her sleeve and can shift from laughing to crying to anger in the span of a single conversation. Victoria speaks to her for nearly twenty minutes before raising a sensitive topic.

"I noted you were once a nurse at the Methodist Hospital in Baltimore, but I also see you have a criminal record. Could you explain that in more detail?"

Wanda smiles and folds her hands in front of her.

"I was addicted to pain killers and started stealing them from the pharmacy. The hospital found out and told the police. Hospital pressed charges and I did eighteen months for it."

"Are you clean now?"

"Five years. I'm taking it one day at a time, but I haven't had any further problems."

"You realize that this is a position where trust is essential, correct?"

"I do, Ms. Wells. I know you got no reason to trust me right off the bat, but I promise I'll do everything I can to show you can count on me."

"I'm sure you will." Victoria extends her hand. "Can you start on Monday?"

Wanda smiles and pumps Victoria's hand. "What was it sold you?"

"These women are more likely to trust someone who's been where some of them have been. You have the qualifications and the shared experience. Plus, I believe in giving people a second chance."

Henry Owens, a young associate at the brokerage firm of Montgomery Trust, exits the elevator on the top floor of the company's offices and heads toward the executive suite. He is moderately tall with short hair. He's dressed in a grey suit with a blue shirt and yellow necktie. He's walking quickly as he has a ten-o-clock appointment with Randolph Ferguson, senior partner with the firm and does not want to be late.

He has been with the firm since receiving his master's in accounting from Columbia University several years earlier. Previously he graduated Magna Cum Laude from Morehouse College in his hometown of Atlanta where he played on the baseball and tennis teams, though not distinguishing himself in either sport. His strengths have always been academic.

He enters the reception area for the executive offices and presents himself to the person at the main desk.

"Yes, Mr. Owens. They're waiting for you."

Worried that he might have gotten the timing of the meeting wrong, Henry heads into Ferguson's office, wondering who else might be in the meeting. The door is ajar and as Henry approaches he hears a woman's voice. This increases his curiosity. He knocks then looks inside. "Mr. Ferguson?"

"Henry, please come in." Ferguson rises and comes around his desk to meet Henry.

"I hope I'm not late."

"Not at all. I told Melanie to send you right in if you were early."

"That's good."

Seated in front of Ferguson's desk is a petite woman with long strawberry blond hair that's French-braided. She's dressed in jeans and a mint-green button-down oxford. Henry guesses that she is in her early twenties. On the floor beside her chair is an expanding file folder.

Ferguson closes and locks his office door then guides Henry to where the woman is sitting. She rises to shake his hand.

"Henry, this is Victoria Wells."

As they shake hands, Henry has the vague sense that

he's met her before but can't recall where.

"Ms. Wells, I've heard a lot about you, especially your philanthropic efforts, but I have to admit I pictured you as much older."

"Looks can be deceiving Mr. Owens."

Henry detects the slight hint of an English accent. Once again, he has the strong sense he's met her before.

Henry sits across from Victoria as Ferguson returns to his desk.

"As you know, Henry, I'll be retiring later this year. For the past few years, I've handled only a few long-standing clients and most of those I've turned over to other associates. Henry, I'm assigning Ms. Wells' account to you. You're an excellent accountant and have proven yourself to be a prudent financial advisor. Ms. Wells and I both believe you'd do a fine job handling her affairs."

Henry doesn't know how to respond. The Wells account has been the subject of much speculation among the associates.

"I'm — I'm honored."

"Now, Henry, I have to caution you that Ms. Wells requires a higher level of attention than any of our accounts and that's why I wanted to meet with you."

"I'm willing to provide whatever services are needed. Honestly, I'm still in shock. I thought an account of this magnitude would go to a much more experienced associate."

"Ms. Wells prefers that the account be handled by a younger associate and once we explain her special circumstances, I think you'll understand why this is important."

"Did the fact that I'm African American factor into this at all?"

Ferguson starts to respond but Victoria stops him. "We compared your résumé to ten other associates with your same level of experience, educational background, and other qualifications, including two other African Americans. If all I wanted was a Black person, there were other choices. You stood out among all of them, Black, white, Asian, and Hispanic."

"Thanks for your honesty. I'll do the best job I can."

Victoria extends her hand. "I'm sure you will."

As he leans in to shake her hand, Henry can't help but catch a glimpse of a scar on her neck. He notes it then looks back to Ferguson who has removed what appears to be a photo album from his desk.

"Glad we got that out of the way. Now for the more difficult topic."

"I don't understand."

"Henry, forty years ago, when I was a young go-getter like you, Mr. Chalmers, the senior partner at the time, called me into his office and introduced me to a client. He then told me a story that I found very hard to swallow, but as time went on, I realized that everything he told me was true. I don't expect you to buy everything you're about to hear right away, but I do expect you to keep an open mind. Deal?"

"Sure thing, Mr. Ferguson."

"Excellent. Now Henry, the client Mr. Chalmers introduced to me was Victoria Wells."

Henry looks at Ferguson in disbelief.

"This Victoria Wells?" He points.

"The same."

Henry shakes his head. "Forgive me for saying this, but I find that very hard to believe." He turns toward Victoria. "I mean, if you're even a day over twenty-five then you look very good for your age."

"You're very kind, and I assure you I am a least a few days over twenty-five."

"Henry, I didn't expect you to believe all of this off the bat. So, I made sure I had this on hand to help prove our case."

He hands Henry the photo album he removed from his desk.

Henry opens it and thumbs through the pages. The first pictures are black and white photos which appear to be from the early- to mid-sixties. The first picture shows Victoria, flanked by a young man and a much older man. Her hands are touching both their shoulders and they're smiling.

"This is you?" Henry recognizes a younger version of Ferguson who nods. Henry looks at Victoria. "And you?"

"Yes."

"That's the day I took over the account from Mr. Chalmers. We'll take similar photos for you to show someone else down the line."

Henry flips the page and there are photos which appear to be from the twenties and thirties and in each Victoria is flanked by a similar combination of older and younger men.

"That's when Chalmers took over the account. That's Stanley Reed the senior partner then. And the last photo is Mr. Reed with Victoria when she opened her first account with Montgomery Trust." He leans onto his desk. "If the photos aren't proof enough, Henry, then let me personally verify that Ms. Wells looks just as young now as she was on the day I took over her account when I was twenty-four."

"This is crazy. Wait."

He flips back to the first photo and this time takes note of the scar on her neck. Flipping back to the older photos, he sees the same scar.

"The scar. It is you. I saw the scar on your neck when you shook my hand. How is this possible?"

"I'm not sure of the mechanics myself."

"Do you mind if I ask—" Victoria stops him.

"If my mother was telling the truth, I was born in Bishopsgate, London, on the day of Queen Victoria's coronation in 1838." Touching her neck. "I got this little beauty in the 1880s and by then I already looked pretty much like I do now and had for several years."

"Wow. So, how long—"

"I have no idea. Just like you. But I expect to be around a very long time. One day, perhaps as a senior partner, you'll hand my account off to another young up-and-comer who won't believe what you're telling him or her."

"So, you can see why a certain level of discretion is necessary when handling Victoria's affairs. And as you might imagine a client like Ms. Wells presents quite a few challenges."

"I imagine so."

"So, from now until the time I retire, I want to devote a portion of my time each day to bringing you up to speed."

"No problem. Ms. Wells, I have a feeling it's going to be a very interesting experience."

Victoria's favorite activity as director of the women's shelter is sitting in on the group sessions where the women talk about their lives and experiences. One afternoon a group of new arrivals are attending their first session and Victoria joins them. As is her custom, she's wearing a Henley shirt with a scarf covering her neck and throat.

"We're happy to have you here and you're welcome to stay or leave as you choose. But be certain that as long as you're with us, we will take every precaution to protect you. Some of you have abusive spouses, boyfriends, or pimps, and we will do everything we can to keep them away from you, but we need your help too by asking you to observe two main rules. Never give out the address or location of this facility. Never reveal the identities of any of the residents to anyone. If there's an emergency, we have other facilities around town and are prepared to get you to one of them quickly. The rules may at times seem overly strict, but in time you'll come to appreciate that they are there to protect you and those around you."

As Victoria is speaking, a young, slender, dark-skinned woman with long tight braids, named Tangie, crosses her arms, and has a sour expression on her face. Victoria continues.

"I know the lives you've led are tough, but we've all been there, and we understand what you're going through."

Tangie gives a loud exasperated sigh.

Victoria looks at her. "Tangie, do you have something to say?"

"Yeah. That's all bullshit. What some rich white bitch know about the kind of life I live?"

Several of the women loudly agree with her.

Victoria looks down, then removes her scarf. "Quite a

bit, actually."

Expressions of shock run through the group. Tangie stares at the scar with a disturbed look on her face. "Damn!"

"Believe it or not, I have been where you've been, feeling like I don't matter, like the world couldn't care less if I lived or died, not even caring myself."

She sits across from Tangie. "I had a mother who drank all day, and told me over and over how much I fucked up her life. A little girl, five, maybe six years old. I suppose I should consider myself lucky, though, because I'm pretty sure she killed my baby sister when she was just a month old."

She rises and points to Tangie. "Do you remember how you lost your virginity?"

Tangie looks down without saying anything.

Victoria points at others. "Anyone?" Receiving no volunteers. "I was staying in a children's shelter, when five or six boys dragged me into a broom closet. One held me down while the others raped and sodomized me. I was ten years old."

She sits then leans forward propping her elbows on her knees. "When I went to report it to the man in charge, he molested me and keep doing it for years until I escaped. After that, I wandered the streets, begging, stealing, and then resorting to the only thing I felt I had to offer anyone. Then one night this guy offered me money to go into an alley with him. Only he had no intention of having sex with me. He strangled me, cut my throat, and left me there to die."

She moves to the seat beside Tangie, who seems disturbed by the story. "They tell me I was dead for a while. I don't remember. There were no lights. No dead family members waiting for me, just darkness. And then the most amazing thing happened. I opened my eyes, and I was still alive. That was when I decided things were going to be different."

There are tears in Tangie's eyes as Victoria continues.

"See, Tangie, I once felt like I was nothing more than a piece of garbage that people used and tossed away. But

then I realized that life had a lot to offer, even for someone like me." She looks around at the others. "That's why,
when I finally had the means to do so, I started this place.
It's a place to come where you can hear people say, you
are welcome. And for some of you it may be the first time
you've ever heard that." She kneels in front of Tangie,
takes her hands, and looks into her eyes. "Tangie, you're
welcome here."

Tangie looks at Victoria a moment then buries her face
in her hands and begins to sob. Victoria embraces her.
"It's okay. You're going to be okay."

After breakfast, Mrs. Mayfair takes Vickie into
London to shop for clothes. They spend most of the
morning trying on dresses and arranging for alterations
and delivery. Finished with the day's shopping, they stop
off at a pub for a light lunch then take a stroll through the
park. As they're preparing to head back in the direction of
Bergeron's, Vickie suddenly stops and presses the knuck-
le of her right index finger against her mouth.

"What's the matter, dear? Did you forget something?"

"More like someone. See I got this friend, Alice. We
was having trouble making the rent and she ain't seen me
since the other night when I came home sporting this."
She touches her neck.

"Is she a good friend?"

"Probably my best friend up till now. I've known her
eight, maybe ten years."

"Do you know where she might be?"

"No idea. She usually stays in at night, what with all the
Ripper business, but she ain't got a steady job. She could
be anywhere."

"Mr. Bergeron will be expecting us back soon. Could
you send her a note — that is, I could write it for you, and
we could get one of the servants to deliver it."

Vickie looks at her with a slightly pleading expression
and says, "Would you mind too terribly if we take a slight
detour? It'd be on the way, just a few streets over."

Mrs. Mayfair shakes her head. "I don't think that's a

good idea. You never know who else you'll run into."

Vickie laughs. "Not to worry. I can handle myself just fine. I'll look out for you."

After a few more minutes of pleading, Mrs. Mayfair reluctantly agrees. They head a few streets over and Mrs. Mayfair can easily detect the point at which they leave the safer confines she's used to inhabiting. Vickie inquires at a few pubs and lodging houses, but no one's seen Alice for at least a day.

"Come on. Maybe she managed to scrape up the rent after all." They turn in the direction of the rooming house that was Vickie's last residence.

As they walk along, two men come up behind them and start to follow them, at first, silently, but as they continue on, they begin calling to Vickie.

"Vickie. Got a moment for an old friend?"

"Just a quick one, Vickie. Wouldn't mind having a go at your friend either."

Both men laugh.

Vickie glances over her shoulder then back ahead. "How are your legs?"

"My legs?"

"For running."

"I suppose I could if I had to."

"You may have to," Vickie says. The men continue to follow them with catcalls and lewd comments becoming more insistent and picking up their pace.

Just then, Vickie pitches her head forward and Mrs. Mayfair looks to see a patrolman strolling along his beat.

"How loud can you scream?"

"As loud as need be."

"Pass me your parasol and once I turn around, stay back behind me. When something happens, scream your head off."

"What are you going to do?"

"Never you mind. Just follow my lead."

Mrs. Mayfair passes Vickie the parasol. Vickie stops and turns, allowing Mrs. Mayfair to get a little ahead of her. She slowly saunters toward the two men. Mrs. Mayfair stops and glances over her shoulder at the patrolman.

"'Ere now fellas. Can't a girl have a few moments to herself once in a while?"

"Come on, Vickie, just a quick one, eh?"

"You want a quick one, do you? All right."

She starts to move toward him, but suddenly stops and jams the parasol into his stomach and proceeds to whack him and his companion with it. Seeing this, Mrs. Mayfair starts screaming and waving her hands. One of the men grabs Vickie's arms and she starts kicking at the other guy while struggling to get away from the first. From down the street a whistle blows and the patrolman, joined by a fellow officer, comes running up to break up the melee.

"Well, look who we have here," the one officer says, holding Vickie by the arm. "If it isn't our old friend Vickie."

Mrs. Mayfair says approaches. "Officer, it wasn't her fault. These men were harassing us."

"And who might you be?"

"I'm Elizabeth Mayfair. I work for Mr. Bergeron at 220 Broad Street."

"Well Mrs. Mayfair. I can take one look at you and see you don't belong here. I don't know what you was doing with this one, but you'd be well advised to keep your distance as she ain't someone respectable people should be associating with."

"Perhaps some respectable people see potential in her. Mr. Bergeron's trying to help her."

The second officer finds this amusing. "Potential to rob you blind."

The first officer concurs. "In any event, she's coming with us as are these fine gentlemen. We'll sort it all out down at the precinct. You tell your Mr. Bergeron if he still wants her, that's where she'll be."

They lead Vickie and the men away.

The program for abused and exploited women at Caring Hands includes numerous self-help and self-awareness workshops designed to encourage the women to overcome the attitudes and tendencies that led them into abusive relationships. Self-defense, self-esteem, and assertiveness training are all part of the mix and while the women aren't required to take any of them, they are encouraged to complete a series of workshops once they've started the first. Along the way Wanda, Victoria, the staff, and volunteers take every opportunity they can to encourage the women and raise their spirits.

One afternoon Victoria's checking the living quarters, when she finds Tangie's children, BeBe and Chet, hanging around outside their door. "Hey guys, what are you doing out here?"

"Mama's crying," BeBe says. "She doesn't like us to see her crying."

"Did she say what's wrong?"

Both children shake their heads. Victoria spots one of the volunteers and motions for her to come over.

"Could you look after BeBe and Chet a little while, Angie? I need to talk to their mom."

Victoria waits until they're down the hall before she taps on the door. She hears shuffling inside and knocks again.

"I'm not ready for you yet."

"It's Victoria. The kids have gone to the activities room."

There's a long pause before the lock on the door clicks and the door opens. Victoria enters to find Tangie dressed in an oversized T-shirt with a pink robe over it and slippers. She's standing by the window with tears on her cheeks.

"BeBe said you were crying. What's wrong?"

"I talked to my great-aunt this morning. She said Lukas was around looking for me."

"You mean the guy who likes to use you as a punching bag. Your aunt didn't say where you were, did she?"

"Lukas doesn't scare her, and he knows it. She told him I left town, and she didn't know where I went. He thinks I went to St. Louis."

"Why would he think that?"

"I used to have family there but not now. He doesn't know that."

"So, you're afraid he'll find you?"

"Sort of. But it just made me think about what's going to happen either way. I mean if he finds me, things are going be bad, but what else I got to look forward to? Find another guy like Lukas?"

Victoria goes to her and rubs her back. "It doesn't have to be like that. You have a great opportunity here. Why not take some of our workshops, talk to some of the counselors. It might give you a better outlook on things."

"What's any of that going to do?"

Victoria puts her hands on Tangie's cheeks and looks her in the eye. "It might help you to believe in yourself. Getting beat down all the time by some man or a parent or society in general is tough. After a while you start to ask what you did to deserve it. You didn't get here overnight. It's going to take some time before you feel comfortable with yourself."

"Maybe."

"You remind me so much of myself, before I stopped caring."

"Why'd you do that?"

"I lost a friend. A good friend to the very same rabble we were trying to escape. After that, I went down a few roads you haven't reached. Believe me, you don't want to go there."

"How do I get away from it then?"

"Small steps, one after another. Before you know it, you've gone a very long way without even realizing it."

"Okay. I'll give it a try."

A day or so later, Victoria enters the activities room. At the far end, Tangie is standing in front of the piano. Tangie runs her hand over the keys then taps out a few notes. Victoria goes over to her.

"Do you play?"

Tangie looks up at her and shakes her head.

"I took some lessons as a kid. But I never had time to learn anything."

"Have a seat."

"No, I couldn't."

Tangie tries to moves away from the piano but Victoria

catches her and guides her back.

"Sure, you can."

She has Tangie sit; Victoria sits beside her.

"Place your hands like this." Tangie places her hands as shown. "Hey, you've got nice long fingers. You should do great."

Tangie laughs.

Victoria shows her some basic exercises and has Tangie repeat them several times.

"You're doing great."

"So, when can I start learning some songs?"

"As soon as you've mastered these. I know it seems boring, but down the road you'll see the difference if you get the basics down first."

They work together for several more minutes before Victoria gets up and pats Tangie on the back.

"You're off to a good start. Work on what I've showed you so far and if you'd like, we can get together tomorrow at 4:00."

Tangie nods and continues practicing.

The following day, Tangie is waiting for Victoria. From then on, they work together every day at 4:00.

When Mrs. Mayfair informs Bergeron about Vickie's arrest, he stares at her for several long seconds.

"Why did you allow her to go to that part of town?"

"I didn't so much allow her as to accompany her. She was determined to go with or without me. I figured she'd get in less trouble if I was there."

"Give me a few moments to ponder this."

"Certainly sir.

She leaves then sits on the top step, where she can hear Bergeron inside the study throwing things around and smashing things. He's also yelling, mostly in a language that sounds like Latin, but Mrs. Mayfair can make out some English sentences. "Low-class whore!" or "Ungrateful bitch. I should kill you again and again and again."

Halfway through the diatribe, Giles appears on the landing below with a tray containing a teapot and some finger food. Mrs. Mayfair gives him a serious face and waves him off. Giles nods and sits on the bottom step after setting the tray on a nearby table.

After ten or fifteen minutes of ranting, Bergeron suddenly gets very quiet. Another five minutes pass before the door to the study opens a crack.

"Mrs. Mayfair, do you know where they're holding Victoria?"

Half an hour later, Bergeron and Mrs. Mayfair, enter the local precinct and identify themselves to the sergeant. "It is my understanding that you have Victoria Seely here. I want her released into my custody right away."

"I'm not authorized to do that, sir. You'll have to talk to the captain."

"I'll talk to the commissioner if necessary. Miss Seely will not spend another hour behind bars."

"Why all the concern?"

"I will only discuss that with someone who has the authority to assist me. Now I want to see that person immediately."

A few minutes later, he's talking to the captain. "Captain, I realize it's easy to look at someone like Miss Seely and see only the bad things about her. I've been guilty of that myself. But I've spoken to her extensively, and she has shown a genuine desire to turn her life around. I realize I'm taking a chance, but I'm prepared to do so if it means helping this young woman live up to her true potential."

"Sounds to me like she was showing her true potential for all to see this afternoon. This isn't the first such altercation she's been involved in and probably won't be the last."

Bergeron presents Mrs. Mayfair to the captain. "Captain, this is Elizabeth Mayfair, who's been a dutiful and trustworthy employee of mine for over ten years, and she is considered by all who know her in the household and around the neighborhood to be an honest and hardworking woman. She's prepared to testify that it was those men who were harassing her and Miss Seely without any prompting from either woman. Any violence perpetrated by Miss Seely was done only to protect Mrs. Mayfair from those two hooligans."

"Is this true, Mrs. Mayfair?"

"It is, sir, as I tried to explain to the constable at the scene."

"Are you aware, Mr. Bergeron, of the unsavory reputation of Miss Seely? She's been on the streets a long time and is not likely to be reformed easily."

"I assure you, Captain, I have plenty of time and patience to devote to the task, and Mrs. Mayfair has agreed to help with the endeavor. You may rest assured that Miss Seely is in good hands and will no longer be a concern of yours."

"All right. We'll release her into your custody. But if she pinches your silverware and makes off in the dead of night, don't say I didn't warn you."

The captain says something to one of the patrolmen and a short while later, Vickie is brought out. She hugs Mrs. Mayfair. "Are you all right?"

"I'm fine, dear. Thank you for protecting me."

Bergeron puts on his hat. "Let's get out of here, Victoria and put this incident behind us, shall we?"

As soon as they get back to Bergeron's home, he excuses Mrs. Mayfair and confronts Vickie in her room.

"Mrs. Mayfair says you were looking for a friend of yours."

"That's right."

"You have no friends outside of this house. Do you understand? To live among the short timers, it's necessary to not draw attention to oneself. Incidents like today are not the way to accomplish that goal. You put yourself at risk, but more importantly, you put me at risk."

Vickie wags her head. "I understand."

"You don't belong to that world any longer. Stay away from any of your old haunts, and do not leave these premises, even with Mrs. Mayfair, unless you have Giles or another male servant with you, is that clear?"

"Very clear. Please tell Mrs. Mayfair I'm sorry for what happened."

"You can tell her yourself."

Mrs. Mayfair returns. "Couldn't we have just ignored those men?"

Vickie pats her cheek. "You know the world you inhabit; I know mine. We had a good walk ahead of us and those boys were getting more worked up as we went. I don't want to think about what might have happened if I hadn't spotted that bobby."

A short while later, some of the dresses arrive, and Mrs. Mayfair spends the afternoon helping Vickie try them on.

Victoria hurries along Houston Street, a few blocks from the shelter. She is responding to a frantic call from one of the volunteers at the center that Tangie's abusive boyfriend, Lukas, had confronted her as she was on her way back from the store. Tangie had run away, but Lukas chased her and one of the women told Wanda who took off after them. They were last seen headed toward Houston Street.

Victoria sees police cars gathered around a lot and she heads toward them. As she arrives, a man she assumes is Lukas is being led away in handcuffs. She enters the driveway but stops when she sees Tangie's body lying at the far end. Wanda is kneeling near Tangie, wailing loudly, and beating the pavement with her fists. Fighting back tears, Victoria identifies herself to the sergeant in charge and he allows her to pass. She runs to Wanda and rubs Wanda's shoulders saying her name.

Wanda looks up at her. "Oh, Vickie. I tried. I tried to get here but I was too late."

"It's okay." Victoria pulls Wanda to her and cradles her. "You did the best you could."

Wanda looks away from her and waves her arm toward the entrance of the driveway. "He was just standing there, leaning against the wall, holding the gun." She folds her arms in front of her. "When the police got here, he dropped the gun and gave himself up. It don't make sense."

"He's going to be held accountable for this. I'll make sure of that. He won't get away with it."

Victoria looks down at Tangie, lying with her head turned slightly toward them, her eyes barely open, blood pooling beneath her, one leg bent, and once again she chokes back tears.

A young officer approaches. "Ms. Wells, I'm Officer Walinsky. The sergeant asked me to tell you that the crime lab's going to need to get in here in a few minutes."

Victoria waves him off. "I understand. Can't we stay with her until they get here?"

"Of course." The officer gives them a sympathetic smile.

"She was working so hard. She was trying to make a better life for herself and— Oh dear lord, what about her children? They got nobody now."

"We'll figure something out."

Victoria's attention is drawn by what she perceives as movement in Tangie's right hand. She focuses on it but doesn't detect anything more. Suddenly, Tangie's right hand begins to twitch then tremble, followed by her left hand.

"Oh, Tangie." Victoria watches her intently.

"What is it?" Wanda looks up and gasps when she sees the movement that's now overtaking Tangie's body.

Officer Walinsky sees it as well and moves toward them. "What in the world?"

Tangie's head starts to twist against her shoulders and her eyes pop open staring ahead. She springs up into a sitting position, takes in a long, deep breath of air and lets out an extended, piercing scream as if every molecule in her body is trying to burst free at once.

Wanda scrambles away from her. "Oh, Jesus!"

Several officers come running, stopping in their tracks when they see Tangie sitting up, shaking, and looking around with a frightened expression on her face. Victoria quickly crawls over to her and puts her arms around Tangie, pulling her close. "It's okay, you're safe now."

"What happened? Lukas! Where's Lukas?"

"He's on his way to jail. He can't hurt you now. You're safe."

"He had a gun. He came at me with a gun—"

Tangie looks around and sees the blood on the ground

and realizes it's also soaking her clothes and screams again.

"Shh," Victoria says in comforting tone while holding her tightly. "We can talk about that later. For now, just know that you're safe."

The medical examiner arrives and is informed he no longer has a dead victim to tend to. The paramedics are called and as they're waiting, Victoria helps Tangie to her feet and guides her toward the patrol cars. Wanda follows them at a distance, still with a confused look on her face. Victoria says to a female officer, "Could you look after her a moment?"

"No!" Tangie grabs Victoria's arm "I want you to stay with me."

Victoria pats her shoulder. "I'll be right back. I've got to talk to Wanda for a moment."

She goes to where Wanda is standing, staring at Tangie, shaking her head. "Wanda, go back to the shelter and do not tell anyone what you saw tonight. If anyone asks, just tell them Tangie was hurt but she'll be okay."

"She was dead." Wanda waves her hand toward Tangie. "I was a nurse. I know what to check. I felt for a pulse and there wasn't one."

"I know. We can talk about it later. Please give the police your statement and go back to the shelter for now, okay?"

"She wasn't breathing!" Wanda speaks forcefully but in a low voice. "Her pupils were fixed. And— and the blood—"

Victoria addresses her firmly. "I know. I really need you to go back to the shelter. There's no one there to look after the others."

Wanda thinks about it a moment then nods. "Yeah – gotta — gotta look after the others." She and Victoria move toward the entrance to the driveway. Wanda hesitates then circles around behind the patrol car away from Tangie. She speaks to the sergeant in charge who takes her contact information and lets her go.

Victoria sits beside Tangie and nods to the officer, who steps away from them. Victoria takes Tangie in her arms and speaks in a whisper. "We have to talk as soon as possible. I have an amazing story to tell you. You and I are more alike than either of us could imagine."

"What you mean by that?"

"We'll talk later. For now, just concentrate on getting better."

When the paramedics arrive, Victoria helps Tangie over to the ambulance then asks them to wait a moment. She approaches the sergeant in charge and pulls him aside.

"Sergeant, I would consider it a personal favor if you could keep what went on here tonight out of the press. This poor woman has been through enough and she doesn't need to be hounded by people who think she's some sort of second coming. I'm not asking you to falsify any official reports, just keep it out of the press."

"Ms. Wells, I don't know what she is. I've never seen anything like what I saw tonight, and I've been on the force for over thirty years." He looks around at the officers. "Jenkins – Sanchez —Walinsky. Over here." He directs them to an area behind the police tape. "These are the ones who were here at the time. Walinsky witnessed the whole incident. I'll have a talk with them, but I can't guarantee anything."

She pats his arm then gives it a squeeze. "Thank you, sergeant. I appreciate anything you can do."

She turns to leave but the sergeant stops her. "Ms. Wells?"

"Yes?"

He leans in toward one ear. "I have a cousin who's on a waiting list for a rehab clinic in Jersey, and—"

"Give me your card." He hands her his card. "I'll call you tomorrow. Caring Hands has several very good facilities around the tri-state area. I'm sure we can find a place."

"Thanks, Ms. Wells."

Despite the concerns of Mrs. Mayfair and the admonitions of Bergeron, Vickie still worries about her friend. A few nights after her incarceration, she devises a plan to check out her old flat without arousing much attention. That night before dinner, she sneaks down into the laundry room where she locates a pair of pants and a shirt and jacket worn by the young teen son of one of the maids, who appears to be about the same size as Vickie.

She sneaks the clothes up to her room and tries them on.

"Little loose, but I'll manage." She hides them then removes from her bottom drawer the one article of clothing she kept when her old wardrobe was discarded, a cap given to her by one of the dockworkers after a few sweaty moments alone in an alley a month or so earlier. He was young and realized after the act that he didn't have as much money as he thought he had. Vickie said she'd take what he had so long as he included the cap. It's a size too large, but tonight, she wants it to ride low on her forehead to conceal as much of her face as possible. Just before she heads to the dining room, she snags a small woolen overcoat and a scarf.

Once everyone is in bed and the house is dark Vickie puts on the boy's clothes and takes out a pair of boots she found downstairs. She pins her hair up then puts on the cap, pulling the bill down to just above her brow line. Finally, she puts on the coat and wraps the scarf so that it covers the lower part of her face. Hesitating a few more moments until she's sure she doesn't hear anyone stirring, she creeps down the stairs carrying the boots. When she reaches the bottom step, she puts on the boots then lets herself out and locks the door behind her.

She moves quickly, her shoulders hunched, and her hands shoved into her pockets. In her right pocket, she conceals a steak knife she pinched from the dinner table. Approaching the rooming house, she slows and surveys the area then moves toward the door. She takes out the key and tries it in the lock.

"Key still works."

Looking around, she becomes aware of a form in Alice's bed. The other two beds appear to be empty.

"Alice." She listens for a response. "Alice, you awake?"

Vickie moves to the bedside table and leans over to

touch Alice's shoulder. She's cold.

"No."

She lights the lamp on the table. Alice is on her side, motionless, her eyes staring and she's not breathing. Vickie sits on the bed she used to occupy and stares at her lifeless friend.

"I am so sorry I couldn't get back to you before now. I brought the rent money." She removes some coins from one of her pockets and holds them out to show Alice. "I guess Kate's taken off as well."

She rises and goes to the part of the room inhabited by the woman she and Alice knew only as Plain Kate, though they never understood why she called herself that. Kate never had many things and apparently what little she had she's already taken out.

Vickie's foot hits something causing it to slide across the floor. She picks it up and takes it to the light to find it's an old, weathered coin with a person's face on one side and a nude man standing on the other. There's what appears to be writing, but Vickie doesn't recognize it. She drops the coin into her pocket then leans over and gives Alice a kiss on the cheek.

"Sorry I couldn't be here for you, my friend. But I'll make sure you get taken care of, I will."

Back at Bergeron's Vickie checks to be sure there are no lights on then unlocks the door. Stepping inside, she takes a few moments to lock the door and remove her shoes. She holds them as she ascends the steps as quietly as possible then enters her room. She drops the shoes beside her bed then goes to the lamp on the nightstand but before she can light it, she is surprised by Bergeron's voice behind her.

"Did you find what you were looking for?"

Vickie jumps then looks into the darkness from where the voice originated.

"Bergeron, what are you doing here?"

"I'll ask the questions. Did you find what you were looking for?"

Vickie considers this a moment then sits. "I found her. She's dead."

"That happens I suppose."

Vickie looks in his direction. "She had her problems, but she was a good woman. She was a good friend."

They are silent for several minutes.

"I suppose you're going to want me to do something for her."

"I wasn't going to ask."

"Still, she was your friend. You'd like to do something, wouldn't you?"

"Maybe a proper burial, with a small headstone. Just so people know that someone cared."

"That can be arranged. Give Giles the information in the morning and I'll have him take care of it."

"Thank you."

Bergeron moves from the shadows toward the window where his profile can be seen. "This is the last of these excursions I plan to tolerate. Your life out there is done. Vickie is dead, do you understand? From now on you are Victoria and you will have no further contact with that life. Any more of this nonsense will cause me to reevaluate if you're worth the trouble."

Vickie faces him. "I've done all I needed to do. Far as anyone else is concerned, I died a long time ago. You'll have no more trouble from me."

"That's good to hear." Bergeron turns to leave.

"Wait." He stops without speaking. "How did you know?"

"I watched you leave. I knew you wouldn't heed my warnings, but I wasn't sure how long you'd wait."

Once he's gone, Vickie puts her hands over her face, leans forward and bursts into loud sobs.

As Henry Owens is at his desk, reviewing a file, Mike, a heavy-set man in his forties walks up and leans over the desk.

"We heard you got the Wells account."

"I really can't talk about that."

"What's the big secret?"

Gladys, a woman with blonde hair, and a thick Brooklyn accent joins them.

"I heard she's a vampire."

Henry rolls his eyes. "I met with her during the daytime. The windows were open. She's not a vampire."

Mike exchanges a look with Gladys. "You met her. Did you see it?"

Henry gives him a confused look. "See what?"

"I hear she's got this really ugly scar on her neck from where somebody tried to cut her head off."

Henry shakes his head. "I didn't ask, she didn't tell."

Gladys presses Henry. "So, what's she like?"

"She's normal — very pleasant. Look, I am not supposed to talk about her. She likes her privacy."

Mike rolls his eyes. "I bet she does."

Gladys wants more. "Come on, Henry, give us something."

Henry takes a long look around then leans toward them. "I'll give you this one thing, but it goes no further, okay?" He looks around once more. "The woman you know as Victoria Wells isn't really her. Well, she is but she isn't."

"What do you mean?" Mike says.

"The original Victoria Wells was an eccentric multi-millionaire who lived in New York for sixty or seventy years. She never married, never had any children, and devoted all her time to doing charitable work."

Gladys nods. "She's famous for her charity work."

"The woman we now call Victoria Wells was originally named Helena Kent and comes from England," Henry goes on. "She's the great grandniece of the original and came here to look after her when she was in poor health. When the first one made out her will, she agreed to leave her entire fortune to Helena, but only on the condition that Helena move permanently to New York, change her name to Victoria Wells and agree to continue—"

From behind him, Mr. Ferguson speaks. "Owens!"

Henry and the others turn to see Ferguson standing there with a scowl.

"A word, please." Ferguson storms into a conference room.

"Thanks a lot, guys," Henry says angrily and joins Ferguson. To those outside, it looks like Ferguson is giving him a major dressing down.

What Ferguson is actually saying as he's angrily pointing and shaking his finger at Henry is, "Do you think they bought it?"

Henry nods dejectedly then bows his head. "If not, this ought to sell it."

"You're lucky," Ferguson says then paces angrily in front of Henry before once again shaking his finger at him. "Chalmers gave me a full dressing down in front of everyone."

"I'll keep that in mind."

"This afternoon, we should start looking at her International portfolio."

"Sure thing." Henry nods with an unhappy look on his face.

He exits the conference room and walks to his desk looking beaten down and defeated. Behind him, Ferguson says, "Consider this your only warning. You won't get a second."

"Yes sir," Henry says dejectedly. He returns to his desk. Mike and Gladys come over and Mike quizzes Henry. "What was that about?"

Henry is emphatic. "No comment. I'd like to keep my job."

That afternoon, Mike and Gladys start spreading the rumor about Victoria to everyone in the office. In less than a week, it has spread throughout Manhattan.

Once Tangie is settled in at the hospital, Victoria heads back to the shelter where she finds Wanda in her office, sitting on the floor rocking back and forth, tears on her cheeks.

"Wanda, are you okay?" Victoria sits in front of her on the floor.

Wanda shakes her head and won't face Victoria.

"Give me your hands," Victoria says, reaching out. Wanda hesitates a minute or so then gives Victoria her hands. At last, she manages to take a quick look at her, before dropping her eyes back to the floor.

"I know what you saw was shocking. But there's an explanation for it."

"How can you explain what I saw out there?"

"Because it happened to me, too."

Wanda pulls her hands away and glares at Victoria.

"What are you telling me? You came back from the dead too?"

"I did. A long time ago when I got this." She touches her throat.

Wanda turns away from her. "How's that supposed to make me feel better?"

"I don't understand."

"All my life, I've been raised to believe in a man who did something no other human being has ever done. He rose from the dead. Now I hear somebody else has done it, see somebody do it right in front of me. What does that leave me with?"

Victoria shakes her head then puts her hand on Wanda's shoulder.

"I don't know what to tell you. I can't help the way I am. Neither can Tangie." She slides over so she's sitting beside Wanda. "As far as the religious aspect goes I'm probably not the best guide because I've never had much use for it."

She takes Wanda's face in her hands and meets Wanda's eyes. "This doesn't have to cause you to lose faith, though. It just gives you more content for it. If your faith is based on a single individual or event, it's on pretty shaky ground to begin with. But if it comes from your own judgment and observations, from your own heart, you can make whatever you want from that." Victoria puts her arm around Wanda and sets her head on Wanda's shoulder. "Don't give up on your faith if that gives you strength. Your church may have given you only one answer and there may be more waiting for you to discover."

Wanda smiles and gives Victoria a hug. "I'm not over this by a long shot but having you around to talk to helps."

"Yeah talk," Victoria says. "I've got to get ready to talk to Tangie when she comes back tomorrow."

"Talk about what happened last night?"

"Worse. I'm going to have to tell her that there's a strong chance she'll outlive her children, no matter how long they live."

The following night at dinner, Victoria is still upset over Alice. Bergeron seeks to cheer her up by letting her know that arrangements have been made for Alice's internment and that while she won't have an elaborate headstone, she will have a modest stone with her name and life dates, if Victoria can recall them. Victoria is grateful but her mood remains low.

As she and Bergeron are waiting for their second course, she removes the coin she found at her former apartment and begins fidgeting with it on the table, tapping it and spinning it.

"What's that you have there?" Bergeron stares intently at the object in Victoria's hand.

"It's a coin. I found it at the flat last night when I went to see Alice."

He holds out his hand. "Let me see it."

She takes the coin to him. Bergeron examines it with extreme interest.

"Do you know what this is?"

Victoria shakes her head. "No, but I can tell it's awfully old."

"I used to carry these when I was a commander in the Roman army in Gaul — which is now mostly France." He holds it up and points to the man's face on one side. "This is Constantine. He's the first Roman emperor who converted to Christianity." He flips over the coin. "This is Sol Invictus, the unconquerable sun. That was Constantine's symbol and his guiding force. It was his vision of a cross appearing on the sun that led to his adopting Christianity."

"What's a Roman coin doing in a rooming house in London?"

"My question exactly." Bergeron hands the coin back to her. She returns to her seat. "Where exactly did you find it."

"It was on the floor over where Kate used to sleep."

"Kate?"

"Yeah, she was the other girl what shared the room with me and Alice. We didn't know much about her, 'cept that she called herself Kate — or, more precisely, Plain Kate."

"She called herself Plain Kate?" Bergeron considers this then says aloud. "Plain Kate, And bonny Kate, and sometimes Kate the curst—"

"What's that then?"

"It's Shakespeare, from Taming of the Shrew."

"Don't know much about that."

"No but you will. In fact, I think that play is in the repertory this season. What can you tell me about this Kate?"

Victoria shrugs then leans on the table without looking directly at Bergeron. "I'd say she was in her twenties. Didn't seem to belong there, so I figured she must not have been on the streets very long. She told us that she'd been living with her father's second wife and her two daughters. After her father died, her stepmom forced her to do all the work around the house while her stepsisters made fun of her."

"That's a child's fairytale. Surely you heard it when you were young."

"Most people I knew back then weren't interested in telling me stories, and those what did, they usually ended up with me in some secluded room or worse."

"What did this Kate look like? You said she didn't seem like she belonged."

"I kind of got the idea she was Irish. Reddish brown hair but very pretty eyes. Gray, they were."

Bergeron leans back in his chair. "How well did you know her?"

"We didn't keep to the same schedule. She was usually around in the early afternoon. Alice probably knew her better, but not by much. Mind you, she was awfully polite, just not too talkative 'specially about herself."

A servant brings in the next course. "We'll talk more about this tomorrow."

Victoria leads Tangie and Wanda into her apartment and closes but does not lock the door behind her. The women take in the whole place for several minutes. Tangie walks over to the window overlooking the park. Wanda examines the photos on the credenza. She picks up a very old looking photo, sepia-toned, of Victoria. "Where did you take this one?"

"Paris. 1893, I think."

"1893?" Tangie walks over to Wanda and looks at the photo. "You got this done at one of those shops where they make old-looking photos didn't you?"

"No, it's genuine. I believe it was Gautier studios. They went out of business in the 20s."

Wanda and Tangie look at one another and shake their heads.

"Grab a seat and I'll get us something to drink."

Wanda and Tangie sit on the couch. Victoria brings in their drink selections with glasses and sets them on the coffee table. She turns a wicker chair so she's facing the couch.

"Are you comfortable?" She gets an affirmative response from the pair. "I brought you here so we could talk about what happened the other night. As I was telling Wanda the other day, I've been through what you experienced that night, but I've never actually seen someone else go through it, so it was a bit of a shock for me as well."

"So, what was it? All I remember is Lukas pointing a gun at me then next thing I know I'm sitting on the ground with you telling me everything would be all right."

Victoria looks at Wanda. "You want to tell her?"

Wanda turns so she's facing Tangie. "When I got there, you weren't breathing. I checked for a pulse and there wasn't one and I shined my little flashlight into your eyes, and they weren't responsive."

"So, what are you saying?"

"You were dead. You'd lost a lotta blood and the bullet

went right through your chest near the heart maybe even right through the heart."

"That can't be right. I'm not dead, I'm sitting here talking to you."

"Now you are, but the other night you was dead. Then it was just like you yanked your soul right back into your body."

Victoria leans forward. "Listen. What I'm about to tell you is going to sound incredible, but it's all true."

She explains about her origins, about meeting Bergeron. She talks about the long-timers and what's she's heard and seen about them. The whole time, Tangie takes it all in with a disturbed look and her eyes pointed to the ground. Wanda also has a disbelieving look but watches Victoria the entire time.

Tangie throws up her hands. "No, no, that can't be. Nobody lives that long. It's just not possible."

Victoria sighs then has a thought. She picks up her phone and dials a number. "Hello, Cassie? It's Vickie. Do you have a few minutes? Could you come to my place, there are some people I'd like you to meet. And if it's handy, could you bring your family album? The door is open so don't bother knocking."

A few minutes later, Cassandra Armstrong enters. She's a medium toned Black woman, average height who appears to be in her late-forties to early-fifties. Victoria gets up when she enters and gives her a hug. She guides Cassandra to a chair in front of the coffee table, introduces Wanda and Tangie then takes her seat back in the wicker chair.

"This is Cassandra Armstrong. She's been living here for, how long Cassie?"

"Since the day I was born, October 4, 1930. My father bought the place, and I got it from him when he passed and raised my family here as well."

Tangie leans toward Cassandra. "How long have you known Victoria?"

Cassandra laughs. "I can't think of a time I didn't know her. She used to give me candy when I was a kid, tutored me in my French when I was in high school and helped me get through all the paperwork when I took over the apartment downstairs."

"And has she always looked like this?" Wanda says.

"She certainly has. When my father first told me about her I didn't think it was possible, but then the years go by and there she is."

Cassandra opens her family album to a shot of her as a child, standing with her father and Victoria in front of the building. "Take a look at this." She turns the album around to show Wanda and Tangie.

Wanda points at the little girl. "That's you?"

"It certainly is."

Victoria looks over Cassandra's shoulder. "That's a great photo of Harold. I may just want a copy of that."

Cassandra pats Victoria's hand. Tangie and Wanda thumb through the album, stopping whenever they come across another photo with Victoria in it. As Cassandra ages in the photos, she begins to resemble the woman sitting across from them.

Victoria steps into the kitchen and returns with a glass and a bottle of diet cream soda. She sets it in front of Cassandra who says, "Aren't you sweet."

Victoria returns to her seat. "Cassie, we just found out that Tangie's like me. She's probably going to be around a long time as well."

"Isn't that something?"

"I'm not sure what it is. What about my kids? Are they like me too?"

Victoria folds her hands and looks down. "I can't say. It's not an exact science just yet, but one man I talked to suspects you have to have a pair of the genes, one from each parent. You may have passed along a pair to your kids, but I'm not sure it even works that way."

"When will I find out?"

Victoria shakes her head. "My experience is that it kicks in between eighteen to twenty-two years old. You're in your twenties right now and will probably look this way for four or five hundred years, maybe longer."

Tangie nearly drops her drink, Wanda stares at her and Cassandra says, "Oh, my."

"How old are you?" Tangie says to Victoria.

"One hundred and forty-seven," Victoria says.

Tangie shakes her head again then holds her hand out. "Are you telling me I could outlive BeBe and Chet? That's not supposed to happen."

"I know, but this isn't really a normal situation," Victoria says. "But if they don't have the right configuration, you could well outlive them, their children and even their grandchildren's grandchildren — even their grandchildren."

"This is crazy," Tangie says. "How will I know?"

"Wait," Victoria says. "That's the most reliable method. See, we found out about ourselves through unusual circumstances. We were both killed and came back. Most people like us don't find out until they've been around a very long time and haven't changed much. If your kids get to age forty and still look twenty then you've most likely got a winner."

"That seems like forever."

"Forever doesn't mean the same for you and me as it does for others," Victoria says. "I wasted the first fifty years of my life. For most that is a lifetime."

She steps into the kitchen then comes back with something in her hand.

"I hate to bring this up, since it was shown to me by the vilest man I've ever known. But there's a quicker method, that's kind of unpleasant."

Victoria holds out her left hand. "Give me your hand."

Tangie places her hand in Victoria's and Victoria takes out a steak knife and holds it against Tangie's hand.

"The test is, I cut you and you watch it heal. But only if you say it's okay."

Tangie meets her eyes. "Do it."

Victoria slices Tangie's hand. Tangie screams and pulls her hand away. Wanda and Cassandra react with shock.

"Now, hold it out and watch."

Tangie does and before their eyes, the cut heals itself in a few minutes leaving no noticeable trace.

"That's incredible," Cassandra says.

"Like I say, it's pretty unpleasant, but definitive."

"I am not about to cut my kids."

"Then time will tell, and you're going to have a lot of that."

"But what am I supposed to tell my kids?"

Victoria shrugs. "If necessary, tell them you'll always be there for their kids and their grandkids."

Cassandra excuses herself and returns home. Victoria answers questions about her past and what she knows about the long timers for Tangie and Wanda for nearly two hours. Finally, she walks them to the door with her arm around Tangie's waist.

"I know this is a lot to take in. But understand that I'm here anytime you need to talk."

"Sure, talk." She hugs Victoria then she and Wanda leave.

Bergeron ascends to his study the following morning and finds Giles awaiting him outside.

"Did you get the papers I requested?"

"Yes sir. They are laid out on your credenza. But, if I may clarify, you did request the theater reviews and not the business section as is your custom."

"That's right. With Miss Seely in the house, I felt it was time I refamiliarized myself with the popular culture."

"Very good, sir."

Giles bows and leaves.

Bergeron takes a seat beside the credenza and retrieves the pile of theatrical reviews Giles has gathered for him. He browses through, first for titles then for names.

"Plain Kate, Plain Kate."

Finally, he stops on an article with the headline, "Austrian Beauty Takes London by Storm."

It's a profile of a young actress named Katerina Fuchs, newly arrived from Austria, who's about to wrap up a celebrated role in a light comedy by Mr. Taylor and is preparing to star in a drama set in the East End. There's no picture with the article, but the physical description convinces Bergeron that she's who he thinks she is. The article also says that Katerina is noted for her role as Katerina in Taming of the Shrew in Austria.

"Fuchs. Hiding in plain sight, eh, Miss Fox?"

He sets the review aside with the intention of proposing an idea to Victoria. When she arrives, Bergeron says, "Was that another shipment of dresses I saw earlier?"

"It was. Am I getting too many?"

"Not at all. You could buy out all of London and I'd have more than enough to send you to Paris and Rome for more. I just thought that perhaps you'd like a chance to show off one of your new gowns tonight."

"What you got in mind?"

"How about a play, a comedy?"

Victoria claps her hands and quickly taps her feet on the floor as though running in place.

"I'd love that! I spent enough time 'round the theaters taking people's wallets, might be nice to go there for the right reasons."

"And who knows, there may even be a surprise or two."

"I like surprises. Good ones at least."

Bergeron sits across from her. "Be ready by six. That will give us enough time to get there by the opening performances."

Despite the best efforts of the police, rumors surface of a young Black woman who died and resurrected on Houston Street one evening. Victoria knows it's only a matter of time before the press finds the police reports which contain a straightforward accounting of what happened even if they can't explain it. The only solution is to get Tangie and her children out of town as soon as possible. Since Tangie has family in Atlanta, all agree that it will be a good place for her to start a new life.

On the day she's scheduled to leave, Tangie finds Victoria in her office and taps on the door. Victoria motions her inside.

"Guess this is it."

"How are things looking for you in Atlanta?"

"Good. My uncle owns several apartments and he's going to let me and the kids stay in one for free until I can get a job. It's not the Ritz, but it's a safe neighborhood."

"Sounds great." Victoria rises and comes around to the front of the desk and leans on it.

"I can't begin to thank you for all you've done for me."

"Me? You did all the work."

"True, but you made me feel welcomed. That's what I needed."

Victoria gives her a long hug. With their arms still around one another, they stop, look into one another's eyes, and Tangie leans in to kiss Victoria. At first, Victoria is hesitant, but then gives into it and they kiss for several seconds. When they finally stop, Victoria looks into Tangie's eyes. "Now why'd you have to go and do that?"

"I've been wondering what it would be like."

"I hope I didn't disappoint you."

"You could never disappoint me. You sure you don't want to make a trip South?"

Victoria laughs then shakes her head.

"I'm not free to make that decision. There's someone here who needs me. Someone I've been with for a long time."

"Story of my life. Whoever this other person is must be awful lucky."

"I'm the lucky one because I know you both. You're going to do great, though. That's who you are."

They hug again then Tangie gives her another quick kiss and Victoria walks her to the door with their arms around one another.

"Stay in touch, okay?"

"That works both ways." Tangie slowly moves away, letting her hand slide down Victoria's arm as she steps through the door, and she grasps Victoria's hand until she's too far away and loses her grip. Victoria leans against the frame of her office door and watches until Tangie turns the corner out of eyesight then returns to her desk and dials a number.

"Yes, this is Victoria Wells. I'm checking on the status of Ruth Marshall."

"Good to hear from you Ms. Wells. Your mother is doing very well."

"Is she eating again?"

"She is."

"That's good to hear."

"She's asked about you a few times. Will you be over soon?"

"Yes, I'll be by later this afternoon. Thanks."

Victoria is having lunch one afternoon with Mrs. Mayfair at a pub in London. Her eyes wander across the space and settle on a dark-haired woman who appears to be staring at her. They make eye contact, and the woman raises her eyebrows then holds up an index finger and moves it to point toward the inside of the café where she also directs her eyes. She looks back at Victoria, then rises and disappears in the indicated direction.

Victoria lays her hand on the table. "I'm going to take another look at the pastries."

"Certainly, dear."

Victoria enters the shop but doesn't see the dark-haired woman and steps over to the pastry counter. "Did a tall brunette just come in here?"

"She went toward the back."

The waiter points and Victoria moves down a short corridor to find the back door is ajar. Victoria pushes it open and exits into the alley, where the dark-haired woman is waiting. She's considerably taller than Victoria. Something about her seems familiar.

"Do I know you?"

"We have never met." The woman's English is clear, but she speaks with an accent Victoria does not recognize. "I saw you going into the house at 220 Broad Street. Why were you there?"

"I live there. What's that to you?"

"I'm acquainted with someone else who lives there."

"Who?"

Something catches the woman's eye. She pulls down the collar of Victoria's dress, focused on the scar.

"Hey!" Victoria swats at the woman's hand to no effect.

The woman releases the fabric. "You're one of us, aren't

you?"

"One of you?" Victoria regards her with puzzlement, then a realization hits her. "Oh. You been 'round a while as well."

The woman nods. "His interest suddenly makes more sense."

"Who are you?"

"Knowing my identity would only cause you trouble. Consider me a friend. One who'll tell you something you've probably already realized." She points to Victoria's neck. "Do not think this will protect you, because it won't. Whenever you make a deal with the devil, you always get burned. Always. He will find a way to hurt you when he's ready."

Victoria eyes the woman for a long moment. She finally dips her head in acknowledgement without removing her eyes.

"I had me doubts. Much obliged, Ma'am."

The woman turns and moves a few steps away. She pauses and looks back to Victoria, who's staring after her.

"The test. You passed."

This catches Victoria offguard. "The test?"

"It's you, isn't it? The one he dreads."

"I don't understand."

"Of course you don't. He may not even realize it himself at this point."

"What are you talking about? What d'you know about a test?"

The woman moves closer and leans in. "Listen to me and listen well. A time will come when you will know what you need to do and when that time comes, do not hesitate. Nothing good will come from second guessing yourself. Do you understand?"

Victoria shakes her head. "No. Not really."

"You will. Just remember what I've said."

She departs, leaving Victoria staring after her.

THE FRENCH DANCER'S WOMAN

Bergeron proposes that he and Victoria head off to Paris for an extended period, maybe weeks, maybe years. She's been studying French and while she's got a grasp of the mechanics, her command of the language is still very unsteady and tentative.

Victoria expresses her enthusiasm over breakfast one morning, but questions one aspect of Bergeron agreeing to take her. "I have always wanted to visit Paris, but what's your motivation for taking me?"

"It's quite simple, really. While the trip will give you the opportunity to practice your French, and expose you to a great deal more culture and history, it will give me the opportunity to introduce the city to you."

"Fair enough."

Mrs. Mayfair and a few other select servants accompany them.

Several days after they arrive, he takes her to the ballet to watch the Danse du Monde troupe perform. Once the dance begins, Victoria watches the action on stage with childish delight. She keeps her eyes trained on a particular dancer, a tall, lithe blonde who dances with much energy and grace.

Bergeron leans over. "We'll be attending a reception afterward. You'll have the opportunity to meet and mingle with some of the performers."

"That'd be lovely." Victoria glances quickly at him then returns her eyes to the blonde dancer.

After the show, they descend into the ballroom where the reception will be held. Bergeron spots someone and seems less than enthused.

"Wonderful. And it promised to be such a lovely evening."

Victoria looks to see an elegantly dressed man and woman approaching. The man addresses Bergeron.

"Bergeron is it that time of the century again?"

The woman picks up the thought.

"We were hoping we'd make it through at least one

ten-decade cycle without the pleasure."

"And you brought a friend." The man doesn't wait for Bergeron to respond and extends his hand to Victoria. "Charles Fox and this is my wife, Renee."

He bows, she curtseys.

"Pleased to meet you." Victoria curtseys.

"And you are?" Renee says.

Bergeron speaks up quickly before Victoria has a chance to reply. "This is my protégé, Miss Victoria Seely."

Charles and Renee exchange knowing glances.

"Bergeron is investing time in someone?" Renee says.

"That can only mean one thing," Charles adds.

"She's part of the family!" they say together.

"Part of the family?" Victoria thinks about it a second, "Oh, you mean you're—"

"We are," Renee says.

"Have been for quite a while," Charles says.

Renee steps beside Victoria and takes her arm. "How long have you been around?"

"What year was that again, Bergeron?"

"Most likely 1838. When Victoria took the throne."

Charles snaps his fingers and points at her. "Hence the name, Victoria!"

"That's right," Victoria says, nodding and smiling.

"Gosh, you're just a kid," Charles says.

Victoria laughs. "That's an awfully funny thing to say about someone who's been around as long as I have. But I guess to you I am."

"You certainly are." Renee puts her arm around Victoria. "Hey boys, I'm going to steal Victoria away for a while to get acquainted."

She winks at Victoria.

Bergeron sighs and looks to Charles.

"And I suppose you'll stay behind to entertain me."

"I'll do my best." Charles breaks into some dance steps, twirls, and strikes a pose with his hands out to his sides and his head tilted.

"Wonderful." Bergeron tells Victoria, "If I'm not here when you come back I'm sure you'll find some way to amuse yourself."

Renee leads Victoria away from them.

"So, you're working with Bergeron."

"Actually, I'm living at his house as well, but not in any kind of romantic way."

"No, that's not what Bergeron usually does with the women in his life. I noticed your accent that you seem to be trying to lose. Did you grow up in the East End?"

"I did, ma'am. Bishopsgate and Whitechapel."

"Whitechapel? That wouldn't happen to be where you met Bergeron was it?"

"Matter of fact, it was."

Renee eyes her suspiciously, leans in and speaks confidentially. "Then I'm going to go out on a limb and guess that you already know you shouldn't trust him."

Victoria looks around to be sure no one is nearby then pulls down the collar of her dress. "I have no delusions, ma'am."

"My god. And you went to live with him anyway?"

"He said he could teach me things. Things it would take me years to learn on my own."

"Yes, I suppose he could. Wait a minute. You passed the test. That's how he found out about you, isn't it?"

"It was ma'am. How I found out about myself too." Renee's mention of a test sparks a memory. "Someone else mentioned a test to me once. She never told me her name, but she was someone like us."

Renee heaves a sigh. "I suppose an evil, insane teacher is better than none at all. I was nearly a hundred and twenty before I started to figure things out and it took me another fifty to realize the implications." She removes a card from under her glove. "Still, I'm going to give you our calling card, just in case you need anything. We have residences in Paris, London, and Florence." She gives the card to Victoria. "We travel a lot, but our solicitor will always know how to find us. I'll give him your name too, so he'll know you're an important contact."

"Thank you, ma'am."

Renee grabs her by both arms and pretends to shake her.

"Enough with the ma'ams! My friends call me Renee,

all right?"

"Sure thing, m— er – Renee."

There's a burst of applause from the door and Victoria looks to see the dance troupe entering. Toward the middle, trailing a bearded man in a tuxedo is the blonde dancer whose performance captivated her. Victoria takes in a deep breath and lets it out quickly. Renee notes her interest.

"So, is that for the bearded guy or the blonde?"

"The blonde. I really loved her performance."

"Why don't you go over and tell her?"

"You think I should?"

"I think you think so." Renee gives her a push.

Victoria giggles, covering her mouth, then composes herself, and heads toward the dancer. As she nears her, the woman looks up and meets Victoria's eyes. Victoria hesitates then smiles and the dancer returns her smile. Victoria starts toward her again, but two men accost the dancer and begin talking to her, blocking Victoria. Victoria looks down and moves away. She goes back to where she left Renee but doesn't see her nor does she see Bergeron. Just then, there's a flourish and an announcer addresses the crowd.

"Mesdames et messieurs, il est mon plaisir de présenter au monde les interprètes célèbres d'Angleterre, Carlton et Carlotta!"

To Victoria's delight, Charles and Renee take the floor in a sweeping waltz. They circle the crowd then come to a stop in the center, and Renee glides away from Charles, while holding onto his left hand. He bows while she curtseys then Renee addresses the crowd. As she speaks in French, Charles repeats what she says in English.

"Ladies and Gentlemen, it is an honor to perform for you tonight in benefit for such a marvelous troupe of dancers. We have prepared a special program for your enjoyment featuring highlights from our recent continental tour. You will witness the very same routines that enthralled all the crown heads of Europe."

The crowd applauds.

Renee takes over the English to Charles' French.

"As you watch tonight, imagine yourself transported to another place and time, a world much simpler, when the values of chivalry and love reigned, when courtly knights wooed chaste maidens, and rode into battle seeking glory and honor. It is our hope that our humble program will entertain the mind, while enriching the soul."

Charles steps away from Renee and says, in French then English: "And now, my lovely wife Carlotta will perform for you a song of enchantment. Of love lost and found. We hope you enjoy."

Renee curtseys then nods to an accompanist behind her. As the music starts, she folds her hands in front of her and begins a song. Victoria is struck by how beautiful Renee's voice sounds. As she's watching, she senses a presence beside her and looks quickly to her left to find the blonde dancer standing there.

The dancer tilts her head slightly. "Bonjour."

Victoria's heart races and she does not quite know what to say, so she nods. "'Ello."

"You do not speak French?"

"I'm learning, but I'm not very good at it right now."

"You should spend some time with a native speaker. You would learn much faster."

"I'll give that a try if I ever run across one."

They both laugh.

"My name is Gisele."

"I'm Victoria. But my friends call me Vickie."

"Then perhaps I should call you Vickie."

"If you'd like."

They listen to Renee for a few minutes.

"Your friend has a beautiful voice. Like that of an angel."

"Yes, but how did you know she's my friend?"

"I saw you standing together before you approached me."

Victoria blushes.

"I didn't get very far, did I?"

"Why did you stop?"

"I saw you talking to those men and didn't want to interrupt."

"I wish you had interrupted. They are patrons. They believe that because they give money they can get whatever they want from the dancers."

"You sound like you're not having a good time."

"I despise these public affairs. Nothing but politics. This is not why I started dancing."

"You're very beautiful up there. I couldn't take my eyes off you."

"You're too kind."

They chat as they watch the performance for ten or fifteen more minutes. During this time, Gisele is repeatedly accosted by admirers.

"How I would love a place where I could hide from all of this."

Victoria looks down then back at Gisele. "I've got a private room not far from here."

Gisele meets Victoria's gaze, and they laugh.

Sally McIntyre is the sort of woman people anger at their peril. A shade under five and a half feet tall and not more than one hundred forty pounds, she has a quick temper and always carries a dagger which she can usually get to in a split second if trouble arises. Her hair is a honey color, long and wavy, and her eyes are two different colors, the right one greenish blue and the left one brown, which always looks down and away from where her right eye is focused. She has a scar on her right cheek from a disagreement with a client who attacked her with a broken bottle in an alley and she has several teeth missing from when another client punched her in the face to avoid having to pay her for services rendered.

Tonight, Sally is lucky because she pooled her money with a friend, and they've gotten a decent room away from the squalor in which they normally spend their days. They're also having a decent meal due to a nice score by her cohort, Vickie, who relieved several theatergoers of valuables including a gold watch fob, a ring, a pair of diamond studded cufflinks, a handful of coins and a wallet filled with pound notes a day earlier. Sally fenced the jewelry for a good payoff and she and Vickie decided to celebrate by spending it all on a weekend fling.

It is a far cry from how their relationship began. Sally was working the theater district picking pockets and learned of another thief who was encroaching on what she considered to be her territory. She didn't know a lot about this other person except that she was small, and her name was Vickie. Sally made it her mission to track down this interloper and teach her what happens to people who fail to respect her boundaries.

It took several days, but finally, Sally spotted a small, red-headed woman working her way along Drury Lane. As Sally watched, the woman accosted a man, and appeared to be asking him directions. What Sally saw, but the man didn't was the woman lifting his pocket watch which she slipped into the pocket of her coat. She thanked the man and moved off in the direction he had pointed.

Sally followed the other woman and about half a block from where the crime had occurred she called out, "Hey you!"

The woman turned and Sally moved menacingly toward her. "You're the bitch what's been cutting into my territory ain't you?"

"There's enough to go around."

The woman turned and started to walk away.

"Stop! You don't invade my territory then just walk away like nothing's wrong." The woman kept walking, and Sally screamed and took off after her. "You bitch!"

They ran around people and carts, through alleys, over bridges. Sally was beginning to get winded when the woman turned into an alley ahead of her which Sally was pretty sure was dead-end.

Sally trotted into the alley but didn't see anyone. She moved along slowly, her eyes scanning the scene. Suddenly someone tackled her from the right side. They both fell to the ground and began wrestling, pulling each other's hair, and whacking one another with their fists or any other object they could get their hands on. After a while they'd worked their way back to their feet and Sally backed the red-headed woman roughly against a wall then went for something under her cloak.

Before she could realize that what she was looking for wasn't there, the other woman snapped her hand up, holding Sally's dagger and pressed it against Sally's throat.

"Looking for this?"

Sally dropped her grip on the woman and backed away with her hands raised.

"You are good. It ain't like I keep that right out where anybody can see it."

The woman still held the dagger in a defensive position. Sally waved her hand. "You won't need that no more."

In response, the woman flipped the knife so the handle was up and handed it to Sally, who waved it away.

"No, you keep it. You earned it."

"Are you sure? You're not gonna need it?"

"I can get me hands on another one pretty quick. Are you Vickie?"

"That's me."

"Yeah, I heard about you. Course, I didn't hear you could handle yourself in a fight, though I guess that stands to reason if you've been out here a while."

Vickie nodded.

"Hey, how's this sound?" Sally moves her fnger back and forth between the two of them. "You and me, we team up, we do. You got the touch; I got the connections. We'd be the perfect team."

"I could agree to that. Fifty-fifty?"

"All right." Sally extended her hand. "Let's shake on it."

In response, Vickie put her arm around Sally's neck and pulled her close, kissing her for several seconds. Once Vickie released her, Sally pitched her head to one side. "Guess it's a deal then."

Sally arrives in their room to find Vickie relaxing in a tub. Hearing Sally enter, Vickie opens her eyes and gestures for Sally to come over.

"You've got to try this, Sal. It's heavenly."

"Maybe when you finish."

Vickie rolls over and props her arms on the edge of the tub. "Why wait?"

"Good question." Sally begins to undress.

Later they are seated at the table wearing only house-coats, feasting on roast pheasant with potatoes and carrots and a good bottle of champagne. Vickie is sitting beside Sally with her head resting on Sally's shoulder. Occasionally Sally feeds her a carrot or morsel of the pheasant.

"Girl could get used to digs like these." She puts her arm around Vickie's shoulder and gives her a long, passionate kiss. "This is all because of you, lover. You hadn't pinched all that gold and those cuff links we'd be on the streets tonight."

"I'm just glad we got to share in it."

They kiss again.

"This is the life. All you need is some rich bloke to foot your bills and it just costs you the occasional tumble."

"I don't know if I could stand it," Vickie says. "Can't think of too many men I've taken much of a fancy to, if you must know."

"That's the best part. You don't have to like 'em. Not liking 'em is an advantage in my book. You don't get so attached so it's easier to move on when the money runs out."

"I guess."

"Now you got the real advantage," Sally says to her, caressing Vickie's face. "You got that young look most men want. Don't matter how old you really are, if they think you're young and tender, they'll pay top dollar they will."

"I never done it willingly before. Had it done to me a time or two and didn't much care for that."

"All the more reason to make some money at it. They take it from you when they can, you might as well take something from them."

Vickie stands holding Sally's hand then kisses and releases it and goes over to the bed. She removes her house-coat and lies on the bed propped on her elbows, facing Sally, one leg bent up.

"I can think of a lot of things I'd rather be doing right now than talking about desperate men."

Sally rises, takes a drink of her champagne then drops

her housecoat and crawls into bed on top of Vickie.

"You're right. This is better."

Allison Stepney was a shy child who grows into an introverted adult, content to live in a world she creates within her head. An artist who studies the people around her, she has a photographic memory and can reproduce on paper just about every detail of a place or object she's seen even if several days, even months have elapsed from the time she's seen it. She's had the best education Cedric and Anne could afford and in school she was a good student, mastering French, Italian, and all her other subjects. As expected, her best class was art.

What is most pronounced about her is the fact that even though she is nearing forty, she has not aged a day since she was in her early twenties. Her friends would joke about it when she was younger, but as she gets older, more and more people in the parish notice and give her odd looks and whisper to one another whenever she's around and go out of their way to avoid her. This causes Allison to withdraw more into her own world.

Given the amount of time she's spent at Stepney & Sons, it's only natural that she works in her father's shop. She spends most of her time away from the shop seated on a bench in the local park sketching whatever or whomever passes in front of her. Her father has always spoken proudly of the tradition he was honoring when he took over from his father. When Allison mentioned taking over the shop someday, Cedric was happy, but also concerned that she wasn't engaging enough with the world around her.

"Nothing would make me prouder than for you to take over the shop, Allie, but you've got to have a life of your own, too."

"How can I have a life of my own when everyone I know thinks I'm some freak of nature? I just want to be like everyone else."

"Allie, you're not like other people."

"But Father, I don't want to be different."

"It's not a matter of wanting it. You have it whether you want it or not. It's a wonderful gift."

"I don't see it as a gift. It's a curse."

"Allie, listen to me. You're not cursed. You were our miracle from the Lord. Right before our eyes you came back from the dead. When the time is right, you'll learn why you are this way, and it will change everything."

The day being somewhat slow, Allison is in the back of the shop, sketching the various coats and trousers hanging around her, experimenting with different lengths, pleats, and cuffs.

From the front, Cedric calls. "Allie, I need you."

She rises and steps through the curtain. At the counter is a distinguished looking man with a van dyke beard and wearing a wool overcoat. A top hat is sitting on the counter. With him is a pretty, dark-haired woman with a creamy complexion and dark eyes. She's wearing a pink satin dress and dark topcoat with a very fancy hat and she's admiring a set of diamond studded cufflinks the man is holding.

"Yes, Allie," Cedric says when he sees her. "This is Mr. Dennert. He's getting a new hat and I noted that we're just out of the right sized boxes. Could you bring some more from the cabinet in back?"

She nods and retrieves the requested boxes.

"Thank you, dear," Cedric says.

Allison steps back and her eyes fall upon the woman. The woman looks in her direction and they make eye contact.

"Comment vous appellez?" the woman says to Allison.

"Allison, ma'am."

"Vous parlez français. Me m'appelle Brigitte."

"Il fait beau de vous rencontrer, Brigitte." Allison gives her a slight smile. Brigitte nods then turns her attention back to her companion.

Allison hangs around awkwardly behind the counter for a few minutes before Cedric notices her still there.

"That's fine dear. You can get back to your drawings if you'd like."

Allison returns to the back and flips to a new sheet

in her sketchbook. She starts drawing the dark-haired woman.

Victoria opens her eyes and rolls to her side and stares at Gisele as she sleeps. The events of the previous evening run through her head, and she cannot believe where she finds herself versus where she was not quite two years ago. Gisele stirs then opens her eyes.

"Bonjour." There's a seductive tone to her voice.

"Bonjour."

They kiss.

"I can't believe you're really here. I keep thinking you're just a vision, and that I'll roll over and you'll be gone."

"I am here, and you are awake, and I am not going anywhere."

They kiss again. Gisele sits up and leans back against the headboard.

"So tell me Vickie Seely, what must one do to have a room like this in Paris?"

Victoria considers the question a moment. "It's less about what I do and more about who I am."

"Then who are you?"

"Someone Bergeron needs right now, and when he needs someone or something, he takes out all the stops."

"And he has never asked you to come to his room late at night or visited you?"

"Never. I think he just wants me around."

Gisele runs her hand over Victoria's cheek. "You are so young."

Victoria laughs. "You have no idea."

"I don't mean age. I mean experience. You have had a limited life up to this point, have you not?"

"I suppose you could say that about parts of my life. Other parts I've had too much experience."

Gisele runs her fingers over the scar on Victoria's neck. "Would this be one of those parts?"

Victoria takes Gisele's hand then kisses it. "That's one, to be sure."

Victoria sits up and lays her head on Gisele's shoulder.

"There's a lot in my past I'm not proud of."

"We can all say that, I believe. But if those experiences helped to make you the person you are now, perhaps it was worth it after all."

"I've never thought of it that way."

She kisses Gisele again.

The door opens and Mrs. Mayfair enters carrying a pitcher and a towel. She freezes when she sees Victoria and Gisele together.

"Oh! Forgive me, ma'am. I didn't realize you had company."

Victoria stifles a laugh as she sits up and props herself on one hand. Gisele is also trying hard not to laugh.

"Mrs. Mayfair, this is Gisele. She was in the ballet last night."

"Pleased to meet you." Mrs. Mayfair tries not to make eye contact. "I just brought you some water for your wash basin." She quickly sets it on the vanity then heads back toward the door.

"Oh, Mrs. Mayfair. Could you tell cook we'd like to dine in 'alf an hour?"

"Certainly ma'am. Well, good morning."

She hurries out.

Victoria and Gisele collapse onto the bed laughing.

"We gave her quite the shock, no?"

"We certainly did. But she'll be all right as soon as she's had time to think it over."

"Are you close with her?"

"Not as close as I am with you right now." This sets off another fit of laughter between them. When she calms down, she says, "But she's probably the nearest thing to family I have right now."

"It's always nice to have someone like that in your life."

Victoria leans in for another kiss. "I could say the same about you."

Later, when Victoria heads down to breakfast, Mrs. Mayfair corners her.

"I'm not going to comment on what you was doing 'cause that's your business. But you should have told me you had somebody with you."

"I am very sorry. It won't happen again."

"See that it doesn't." Mrs. Mayfair shakes her finger at Victoria then changes tone. "She's a right pretty girl, she is."

"She's beautiful." Victoria can barely contain her joy.

"Will you be seeing her again?"

"Almost certainly."

She winks at Mrs. Mayfair.

At dinner, Bergeron keeps his eyes trained on Victoria the entire time they eat. "I understand you had a guest."

"I did. Do you mind?"

"Why should I mind? You're free to spend your time with whomever you want. But let me give you a word of warning about getting too close to them."

"Them?"

"The short timers. They're fine for an occasional dalliance, a brief fling, but don't get attached."

"Why shouldn't I?"

"Because you'll always lose them. Use them for whatever purpose you need then discard them because either way, it won't last."

Victoria runs this around in her head. "I think I'll take my chances."

"Go ahead. Sooner or later, you'll learn."

Brigitte Marcal has not been having a pleasant evening. She's just attended a show with Dennert, one he is producing and in which he hopes to integrate her. Dennert has also made it clear that before that happens he plans to integrate himself into Brigitte. She likes Dennert well enough, but she can think of many more things she'd rather do than spend time rolling around in a bed with a fat, sweaty, and drunk show producer, who, if he were the age he looks, would be old enough to be her father but who's closer to the age her grandchildren might be if she had any.

As Brigitte exits the theater, she sees Dennert accosted by a small, poorly dressed woman who first grabs him by the left wrist and forearm and seems to be pleading with him for something. Dennert shoos her away, but she crosses in front of him and grabs his right wrist and again seems to be intensely begging him for something. Dennert yells at her to get away from him then roughly pushes her aside, causing her to lose her balance and fall to the pavement. Dennert boards the carriage.

Brigitte shakes her head then walks over to the woman, who's sitting on the pavement, and offers her a hand.

From the carriage, Dennert yells in French.

"Brigitte! Get in here this instant or I'll drag you in!"

Glaring at him over her shoulder, Brigitte spits out her response in French.

"If you plan to see any more of me than my face tonight, you'll keep your fat ass in the carriage and shut your mouth."

The woman takes Brigitte's hand and stands. Brigitte notes that the woman does not appear to be very old and there's something familiar about her that Brigitte can't place.

"Much obliged, ma'am."

"I apologize for my escort. He likes to push the ladies around, perhaps to make up for certain inadequacies on his part."

She takes some bills from her purse and gives them to the woman. As she does she notices something in the woman's hand and looks to see the woman is holding a pair of diamond studded cufflinks. Brigitte looks up, meets the woman's eyes.

"What is your name?"

"Vickie, ma'am." The apprehension in her voice is apparent.

"Have a pleasant evening, Vickie." Brigitte gives her a grin then goes to join Dennert.

Vickie returns the grin. "You as well, ma'am."

As she boards the carriage, Brigitte gives Vickie one last glance as she strolls away, hands in her pockets.

Gisele takes Victoria to a rehearsal at the theater. It is a revue, featuring dance, song, and drama and Victoria is pleased to see Charles and Renee Fox are part of those gathered.

"Victoria!" Renee embraces her then indicates Gisele. "I see you managed to speak to her."

Victoria blushes. "Actually, she spoke to me first."

Gisele puts her arm around Victoria. "I could not resist."

Charles has been on stage reading a script, but seeing Victoria and Gisele, he jumps down to the aisle and approaches.

"The mood in here just lightened considerably."

"They arrived together." Renee speaks conspiratorially.

Charles looks over both. "I'd be hard pressed to say which is the luckier of the two."

Victoria blushes again then walks toward the stage. "So, this is what a production looks like. Makes me wonder how you pull it off."

Gisele, Charles, and Renee follow behind her and Gisele says, "I assure you it is not magic."

"That's right," says Renee, "it takes a lot of hard work and practice."

"Will you be singing, Renee?" Victoria turns back toward them.

"I will if my accompanist ever shows up. He's late again and I'm starting to get annoyed."

Charles mimics the actions of someone drinking then winks at Victoria.

"You wouldn't happen to know anyone who can play piano would you?" Renee says.

Victoria shrugs. "I've been taking lessons."

"Have you now?" Charles looks at her sideways. "A hidden talent perhaps?"

"I don't know if I'm all that good. I've only been studying for a couple of years."

Renee hands her a sheet of music. "Can you read that?"

Victoria looks it over. "I think I could follow it."

"Let's give it a try." Renee guides Victoria to the piano.

Victoria sits and runs a few scales up and down the keyboard to test the sound. "Nice and tuned!"

She looks at the music and taps out a few of the notes.

Then begins playing with almost no breaks or missed notes.

"Impressive!" Charles says. "You sure you've only been studying a few years?"

"Absolutely, but my instructor tells me I learn quickly. I guess it's because I enjoy it so much. I practice all the time."

Renee pats her on the shoulder. "Well you keep it up and you may just end up in the show yourself."

Forty minutes later, a plump, bearded man stumbles in and heads for the piano. Renee sighs and crosses her arms.

"Edgar, so nice of you to make an appearance. Did you bring the new pieces?"

"No madam. I have not had a chance to get home."

"I see. Then you're fired. You'll receive payment through the end of the day and don't even think about getting a reference."

"You have no authority to fire me. I work for the theater."

"Your contract is with me, not the theater. Feel free to plead your case to whomever you please but do it elsewhere. You will not play for me again."

He makes an obscene gesture then stumbles out.

"Well, that was hardly called for," Charles says.

Renee shakes her head then puts her arm around Victoria. "Looks like it's you and me, kid."

Victoria is nervous. "I don't know. I've never performed in front of an audience."

Gisele takes her hand. "Please say yes. Then you and I can be in the show together. Perhaps you can play for me as well."

Victoria looks around at Renee, Charles, and Gisele, all of whom are watching her with anticipation.

"I'll give it a shot."

"Great" Renee says. "Let's get started, shall we?"

As Victoria expected, Bergeron is not happy to hear of her participation in the revue.

"You should steer clear of the Foxes. They're a bad influence."

"Bad influence? You cut my throat within a few minutes of meeting me. What more could they do, set me on fire?"

"They're show people. What they do looks like fun, but society doesn't think much of it."

Victoria rolls her eyes. "They've only asked me to play piano for one evening's performance. Didn't you tell me you wanted me to immerse myself in the culture?"

"I meant as a spectator, not a participant."

Despite Bergeron's protests, Victoria continues to rehearse with Renee for the show. She's featured in two spots, first with Renee singing solo then for a piece featuring Renee singing as Gisele dances. For this one, Victoria must concentrate to be sure she pays attention to the music and doesn't watch Gisele. Not an easy feat for Victoria.

In the weeks since they met, they've arranged their schedules so they have the same time off and spend as much of it together as they can. They roam the streets of Paris, arm in arm, visiting galleries, cafes, and the latest clubs. Victoria worries that Gisele might tire of her, but Gisele never seems bored or at a loss for conversation. They alternate between staying at Gisele's flat and Victoria's room at Bergeron's though Victoria generally suggests they not remain there very long for reasons she's reluctant to share with Gisele.

Each afternoon, they end up at the theater, where they continue to prepare for the revue. Victoria has learned both pieces very well, so much so that she can almost play them with her eyes closed, which is a good thing, since she still tends to gaze at Gisele whenever she's onstage.

The night of the performance, the house is packed, and Victoria is especially nervous. Gisele comforts her. "You will do fine."

Looking out over the crowd, she spots Bergeron in the audience and thinks, *That's odd. What's he doing here?*

Renee is pacing backstage humming her first song to herself. Charles walks by and pats her on the shoulder.

"Break a leg."

"And a couple of ribs, too."

The curtain goes up and the first act goes on. As they finish, Renee looks at Victoria and nods. Gisele hurries over and gives Victoria a quick kiss then heads back to the dance troupe who'll be performing after Renee's first number. The master of ceremonies announces her, and she glances at Victoria. "Here we go."

As she's sitting down at the piano, Victoria realizes she brought the wrong piece with her. She panics briefly, but steadies herself.

Stop this, you know it. Now play.

Renee nods to her and she begins. As she plays, she forgets all about where she is and what she's doing and concentrates on the music. She occasionally glances at Renee to see if she's giving any cues, but Renee sings to the crowd without concern. When they conclude, Renee bows then waves her hand toward Victoria who stands and curtseys. Backstage Renee gives her a big hug.

"You were great! You kept right with me with just the right tempo."

"Pretty good, considering I took the wrong music out."

"I never would have known."

Charles comes over and gives Victoria a hug. "You did good kid. Keep this up and you'll be turning away singers left and right."

The announcer introduces Danse du Monde and Victoria goes to the wings so she can watch Gisele. As always, Victoria can't take her eyes off her as she dances. At one point, Gisele glances over and gives Victoria the slightest hint of a smile. Once du Monde is off the stage, Gisele hustles into wardrobe to change for her number with Renee. There are two acts in front of them.

Of the two pieces, Victoria is more nervous about the second one, not because of Gisele, but because there are several stretches where she's playing solely for Gisele, so her performance will be highlighted more than when Renee is singing over her. Shortly before the performance, Gisele joins Renee and Victoria in the wings. She wraps her arms around Victoria and gives her a hug.

Renee glances at them. "Break a leg." She looks again at Gisele. "Figuratively speaking, that is."

There's a long musical introduction before Renee begins and even though Victoria brought the correct music, she hardly looks at it as she plays. Gisele is to begin dancing just before Renee comes in and Victoria reminds herself once more to concentrate on the music not the dancing. Before she's even aware of it, she's playing the closing bars, and the crowd begins to applaud.

Once they're backstage, Gisele wraps her arms around Victoria and gives her a long kiss. "Tu étais magnifique!"

Renee and Charles are there congratulating her as well. The rest of the show goes well and before long, Victoria and Gisele are leaving with Charles and Renee.

"I say we celebrate," Charles says. "Our place isn't far from here." To Victoria: "Think your landlord will mind you being a bit late?"

"Oh, I've had nights out before. He'll be fine. Did you notice he was in the theater?"

Charles ponders this. "He never struck me as the theater type."

It's very late when Victoria finally makes it home. As she ascends the stairs, she notices a small table set up beside her door. Reaching the second-floor landing, she finds a vase with some roses in it and a card.

The card reads: "Glad to see the lessons are paying off. —B."

Gisele and Victoria are lying in bed at Gisele's flat, Gisele sitting up and leaning against the headboard and Victoria resting her head on Gisele's shoulder. They have, for the past hour, been avoiding the subject they know they must confront, but neither is quite ready to bring it up.

Finally Gisele kisses Victoria's forehead and says, "It will only be for a few months. Hardly any time at all."

"At least six months. Then you'll be getting ready to go to America."

"I promise you I will make time for you when we're

back."

Victoria sits up and draws her knees up to her chest and wraps her arms around them, setting her head on her knees.

"That's just it. Bergeron's already making noise about returning to London. He wants to get me away from Charles and Renee. He says they're a bad influence."

"Why does he have such a problem with them? They are the nicest people I've met. They're not nearly as vain as some of the actors I've encountered. Why would anyone have a problem with them?"

"You don't know Bergeron. He has a problem with just about everyone. But with Charles and Renee it's personal. See I think they go way, way, back and have a bad history between them."

"Some people are like that. I am glad he does not have a problem with me."

"He probably does." Victoria takes Gisele's hand and kisses it. "He just won't say anything around me."

"Well forget him. When this tour is over, you can come here and live. We don't need much room and I enjoy being close to you anyway."

Victoria gives her a peck on the cheek. "So what's the first stop on the tour?"

"We go to Lyon first as a sort of tryout then it's off to Munich. From there we work our way through Germany to Copenhagen, Hamburg, and Amsterdam, finally ending in Brussels."

"Too bad you're not coming to England."

Gisele pulls Victoria to her and lays her head on Victoria's.

"Yes, I know. I would love for you to show me the city you know."

"I doubt you'd want to see most of that London. I hardly want to see it myself anymore. But I'm sure we could find some mischief to get into."

They start to laugh. Gisele is suddenly seized by a fit of coughing.

"Are you okay?" Victoria rubs her back.

Gisele takes a sip of water. "Yes, yes I'm fine. I suddenly

had a tickle in my throat."

"You've got to stay healthy, my love. As demanding as your routine is, I'd hate to think of you trying to do it if you weren't at your best."

"I'll be fine." Gisele grasps Victoria' hands. "And this tour will pass quickly. We'll write one another often, so it won't seem so bad."

The news spreads quickly throughout the East End that Sally McIntyre has been murdered. The details are sketchy, but the general rumor is that she tried to rob a client and he responded by beating her to death. A crowd gathers outside the rooming house where the incident occurred, hoping for a glimpse of the blood and gore. The coroner's wagon is there and soon a stretcher comes out bearing the body of the slain woman, uncovered, her clothes ruffled and torn. Her face is almost unrecognizable, and her hair is soaked with blood. The crowd reacts with shock at the sight.

On the outskirts of the crowd, Vickie mills about, anxiously watching the door to the establishment.

Soon the police emerge with the suspect and walk him toward the paddy wagon. His fists are bruised and bloody and he's heavily intoxicated. The crowd presses forward, surrounding them, making it difficult for the police to get him to the wagon.

Halfway through the crowd the man cries out in pain and his knees buckle, then he drops to the ground. Blood spurts from a wound to his neck but slows to a trickle a minute or so after he falls. A few feet away, another officer retrieves a bloody dagger lying on the sidewalk.

Nearly a block away, Vickie walks quickly from the scene, her hands shoved into her pockets. She pauses briefly to look over her shoulder at the chaos behind her.

"Burn in hell, murderin' bastard."

For the first month or so after Gisele leaves for the tour, she and Victoria correspond almost daily. As time goes on, the letters slow to twice a week then once a week and finally, Victoria's most recent letters go unanswered. Each day she checks the mail for a response and each day she returns disappointed. Victoria consoles herself with the thought that the tour is keeping Gisele too busy.

Since returning to London, Victoria has had almost no contact with her friends from Paris. Though Charles and Renee have a home in London, they've gone abroad for a tour of America and won't be back for nearly a year. Bergeron frowns on Victoria having any further contact with them and while he doesn't say anything, she can tell by his attitude at dinner that he's pleased that the "bad influence" has been removed from Victoria's life.

One afternoon while returning from the bank, Victoria spots a familiar face from Danse du Monde, a dancer named Claude. She greets him and asks why he's in London.

"We are preparing for our American tour, and I needed to wrap up some affairs first."

"That must be exciting. I've never been to America, but perhaps I'll get there one day." Victoria hesitates a moment then asks the question she's been burning to know. "I imagine the preparations are keeping you busy. I haven't heard from Gisele in quite a while."

He gives her a curious look. "But Gisele has not been with the troupe for several months. I thought you would have known."

"No. What happened?"

"She fell ill during our tour. At first she would start coughing and couldn't seem to stop then she began losing her strength. Finally, the director insisted she return home. A few days later, they hired a new dancer to replace her."

"Why wouldn't she tell me? Do you know where she is now?"

"I am friends with the new dancer, Brigitte, and she tells me that Gisele is at her flat but does not look very well."

Victoria squeezes his arm. "Thank you so much for telling me."

"As I say, I thought you knew already. I hope she is being cared for wherever she is."

"She will be. I guarantee that."

Bergeron is not pleased at the prospect of Victoria leaving London again, but she insists, and he finally relents. The following morning, she boards a boat for France.

In her early rehearsals with Danse du Monde, Brigitte feels she has returned from exile. When she left Dennert's dance troupe several years earlier, Dennert let it be known that anyone who hired her would find it difficult booking venues in Paris. As he was the owner of most of the venues, the troupes took him at his word and refused Brigitte so much as an audition. Since then, she's drifted between London and Paris, dancing whenever and wherever she could, often under an assumed name and in some less than respectable places.

At last, she received word that Dennert had choked to death while in the company of one of his mistresses. His wife, Frederica inherited all his holdings and immediately sold them piece by piece until she had enough cash to retire to the South of France with her young lover, another of Dennert's dancers. Brigitte waited a few months then once again began auditioning. When word reached her that Gisele Bourgeois had fallen ill, Brigitte didn't wait for the troupe to return to Paris, but immediately left for Stuttgart, where Danse du Monde was performing and booked an audition.

While she's happy for the opportunity to dance with a respected company again, she regrets not being able to dance with the woman who many believed to be the greatest dancer of her generation. Several months later, at their final performance in Brussels, the director informs the troupe that in addition to their U.S. tour, they've been invited to perform at some sort of exposition in the southern United States late in the year. They return to Paris the following day.

As they're entering the theater, Brigitte spies a woman standing some distance away watching them. She is taller than average with unkempt blonde hair and dark circles under her eyes. She's pale and looks unhealthily thin. Still, Brigitte can see that she once was a very beautiful woman, and she still carries herself with grace and dignity. She's wearing a faded dress with a shawl around her shoulders which almost seems to weigh her down.

Most of the dancers appear to know her, but some react with expressions of disgust, while others wave, but with tears in their eyes. To these, the woman nods or waves back. The director looks harshly at the woman but makes no attempt to approach or speak to her.

"Who is that?" Brigitte asks the director.

"That is Gisele."

"My god. She has deteriorated that much? Why is she standing over there?"

"She has been told to stay away from the theater."

"Why?"

"She has the plague. Now go inside."

Brigitte gives him a long glare then starts toward Gisele. The director grabs her arm. "Brigitte, go inside."

She swats his hand away. "Touch me again and I will cut your arm off."

The director throws up his hands and goes inside locking the door behind him. Brigitte goes to Gisele, who's now sitting on a bench, looking totally exhausted.

"Excuse me. You are Gisele Bourgeois."

"Yes. Are you not afraid I will infect you too?"

"I am not worried." She sits beside Gisele. "I am Brigitte Marcal. I replaced you in the troupe."

"I have heard your name before. You were with Dennert, were you not?"

"Yes. In more ways than I care to remember."

This amuses Gisele.

"I have known most of the dancers in du Monde for many years. I recommended the director when the previous one left. Why is it you are the only one who will come speak to me Brigitte?"

"You are sick, that is not your fault."

"You do not believe I am cursed? That is what people say about me when I walk by them. I am not allowed to go to the market. If I did not already own my flat, I have no doubt I would be evicted from there."

"People are fools." After a moment, she looks over Gisele. "Do you have someone to stay with you?"

"I manage."

"But do you have anyone?"

"My brother Davide is stationed in Algiers and cannot come home. Our parents are dead."

"Have you told your brother about your condition?"

"He could not come even if he is told. I do not want him to worry about something he can do nothing about."

"You should let him know He may be able to help you even if he cannot come himself."

"Our family's finances were ruined before our parents died. All that is left is the house and that is in Davide's name. We do not even have the money to afford servants. That is why he had to accept a commission with the Legion. Before I became ill I was making more than he is currently. Perhaps I should not have spent so much of it."

"You had no way to know."

Gisele rises. "I should return to my flat. I came down here hoping to see all my friends. Instead, I found just one I did not know I had."

Brigette stands. "How far is your flat?"

"Not far."

"May I walk with you."

"Of course."

When they arrive at Gisele's apartment, Brigitte helps her up the flight of stairs and into her room. Brigitte rummages in the cabinets and finds some bread and cheese and some vegetables then starts a fire and puts on a pot of water. Into it she puts some carrots and celery and some potatoes.

"You really do not have to," Gisele says. "I can get that."

"Let me help you. That is what friends are for, no?"

Once she's gotten Gisele set up, Brigitte prepares to leave. "I am afraid I must go. I need to see if I am still dancing for du Monde."

"I hope I did not cause you any trouble."

"None of it is your fault. If I lose my place in the troupe because of this then perhaps I am better off after all. You take care of yourself."

Gisele rises and extends her hand. Brigitte puts her hands on Gisele's shoulders and leans in to kiss her on each cheek then she hugs her tightly. There are tears in Gisele's eyes when Brigitte looks at her again.

"Merci, Brigitte."

Back at the theater, Brigitte finds the door still locked. The director comes when she knocks, but speaks through the door.

"You will not bring that sickness in here. Go home and change your clothes and take a bath."

He disappears inside again.

Brigitte stares after him a moment, then turns and walks away.

"The sickness is already in there."

Several weeks after meeting Brigitte, Gisele is returning from the market with a small bag of groceries. While the owner won't allow her to enter, he will collect items she requests and deliver them to her at the curb where she pays him.

"I have no problem with you coming in, but my other customers have threatened to take their business elsewhere, if I allow those who are sick inside."

As she walks along, she's overcome by a fit of coughing and holds a rag over her mouth. There are flecks of blood on the rag as she places it back into her pocket. She recalls how short the distance to the market seemed before, when she was in good health. Now it seems like many miles, and she must stop every few steps to catch her breath. Today she seems especially tired, and she has not eaten as well as she should have. After several more steps, she stops and sets the bag down and leans against a wall, trying to draw in enough breath to build up her strength again.

Suddenly a hand reaches down and takes up the bag. Before Gisele can say anything, she feels an arm around her waist and she looks to see Victoria there, holding the bag in her arm.

"Put your weight on me."

"Why are you here? I do not want to make you sick."

"I don't get sick. Now put your weight on me, let's get you home."

Back at Gisele's flat, Victoria puts the groceries on the table and helps Gisele over to the bed. She sits beside Gisele. "I'm here as long as you need me."

"You should go before you get sick too." Gisele looks away from her,

Victoria puts her hand on Gisele's cheek and gently moves Gisele's face back toward hers and presses her lips against Gisele's. "I told you; I don't get sick."

Gisele breaks down, laying her head on Victoria's shoulder.

"I am glad you are here. I have been so alone. My friends have abandoned me, and my brother cannot come."

"Have you told him?"

"No. He is in Algiers and cannot get back. I do not want him to worry."

"I'll write to him. I'll let him know that I'm with you and will look out for you until he can make it back. Why didn't you tell me?"

"I could not. I was afraid I would infect you. And I did not want you to see me like this."

"You're beautiful, my love. You'll always be beautiful to me."

"You are so kind. I do not deserve someone like you."

"You deserve so much more than I can give you. When was the last time you ate?"

"This morning. I had some bread and cheese."

Victoria kisses Gisele's cheek. "Let's see what I can whip up for you."

Victoria is sitting on the edge of the bed with Gisele resting her head on Victoria's shoulder. Victoria has one arm around Gisele's shoulders the other is holding Gisele's hand.

"There's something I need to tell you about me."

"You can tell me anything."

"It's going to sound unbelievable."

"Is it true?"

"Yes."

"Then if you tell me it is true, I will believe you no matter what you say."

Victoria tells her about Bergeron, the attack, her life span and why she doesn't get sick. Gisele listens without reacting.

"That is an incredible story. I knew there was something special about you when I met you. Now I know there is something more."

"I wish I could give it to you, my love, even if it meant me losing my own life."

Gisele places her hand over Victoria's heart. "If you will always keep me here then I will never die."

Victoria places her hand over Gisele's. "You don't even have to ask."

Gisele looks into Victoria's eyes. "Then maybe I will live forever as well."

Gisele drops off to sleep and Victoria takes the opportunity to go to the grocers and also post an important letter. When she returns from her shopping excursion she puts the food she's purchased on the table. Gisele is sitting up but is leaning against the headboard and appears to be sleeping.

"I am glad you are back," she finally says, in a weak voice. "I feel better when you are here."

"I won't leave again." Victoria puts away all the items except what she plans to prepare for lunch. She takes a quick look at Gisele. "I've sent for Davide."

Gisele gives a slight laugh and leans her head back. "Then it will not be long will it?"

"No." Victoria sits on the bed and then holds Gisele's hand in her lap.

Gisele speaks in a raspy voice. "Promise me that you will think of me from time to time,"

Victoria puts her arms around Gisele, holding her tightly.

"Tu vivras pour toujours dans mon cœur."

Gisele gives a slight laugh, stifling a cough.

"You see? All you needed was to spend some time with a native speaker."

By the time Davide arrives at his sister's flat, the room has grown dark, but there is still enough light for him to see a small woman on the bed, holding Gisele close to her.

He removes his hat. "Bonjour."

"Bonjour."

He lays his hat on the table and steps to the foot of the bed.

"Je suis Davide, le frère de Gisele."

"Oui." The woman replies without looking at him.

He notes her expression then looks at Gisele. "Est-elle morte?"

"Oui."

"Combien de temps?"

"Elle a cessé de respirer il y a une demi-heure. Son cœur est arrêté après ça."

Davide looks down and away from them, covers his eyes. "Alors je suis trop en retard."

The woman addresses him in English with a Cockney accent. "She knows you tried. That's all that matters."

Davide looks at her again. "You are Victoria."

"That's me."

"Your updates have provided me with much comfort, knowing my sister was receiving good care. Gisele mentioned you many times in her letters as well. You were very special to her."

"She's special to me as well."

Davide pulls a chair over and sits.

"Are you staying nearby?"

Victoria shakes her head. "I've been staying here."

"You weren't worried—"

"No. She's all I was worried about."

He leans toward her.

"I have some people downstairs. They can take care of her now. Will you accompany me to my family's home? You will stay there as my honored guest."

Without speaking Victoria gently lifts Gisele away from her and lowers her onto the bed. She rises then leans over and kisses Gisele.

"Sleep well, my love."

Davide gets his hat, and she gets her hat and coat. He offers her his arm. She nods giving him a slight smile, takes his arm and they exit.

Victoria has been at the Bourgeois home for a few days when she finds Davide in his study, his hands pressed against his forehead, very upset.

"Davide, what's wrong?"

"The priest. Father Barone is refusing to allow Gisele to be buried in the churchyard. Generations of our family are there as well as our parents. Gisele should be with them."

"Why would he refuse to let her be buried there?"

"He tells me her sickness was evidence of God's judgment upon her. I am certain, though, that he would have found a reason to object anyway."

"Why on earth would he do that?"

"There are many fine priests in the church who live in this century. Father Barone is not one of them. If he knows of the work of Pasteur he no doubt dismisses it as meaningless or the work of Satan. He follows a strict doctrine, sees natural events as signs from the Lord. He speaks often of visions and dreams which guide him. He sees individuals as nothing more than worthless sinners."

"That's ridiculous. Gisele was the most beautiful and talented person I've ever known."

"Yes, but her work in the theater was enough to condemn her in his eyes. She did not seek the company of men, nor did she wish for a family. In his mind, that was against God's commandments. Her illness was, for him, a sign of God's disapproval."

Victoria looks away from Davide.

"Believes in signs, does he?"

A short while later, Victoria enters the church and approaches Father Barone speaking to him in French. "Father Barone?"

He turns. "Yes, my child."

"May I have a word with you? I would like to discuss Gisele Bourgeois."

The priest frowns.

"That matter is closed. She cannot be buried in the churchyard."

"What reason would you have to keep her from being buried with her family?"

"She flaunted her degenerate lifestyle before God without concern for her immortal soul and died with the full weight of her sins upon her. God rendered his judgment when he struck her ill."

"If that is so, why did I not get sick? I was with her every day for months. She coughed on me, bled on me, yet I stand before you in perfect health."

"Perhaps it is a message from the Lord for you to change your ways." He turns away from her.

Victoria becomes very agitated. "Maybe the Lord is trying to talk to you, too."

Barone turns back to her. "Madam, I speak with the authority of the church." He raises his hand toward the large crucifix behind the altar. "Which speaks with the authority of our risen Lord."

"Risen Lord? Is that what it takes? If that is the case, then I have ten times your authority." She unbuttons her blouse and pulls it open, revealing the scar on her neck. "I rose from the dead too!"

Father Barone recoils as he stares in horror at the scar. He backs away until he collapses onto the altar.

"Demon! What do you want of me?"

"I'm no demon." She walks slowly toward him. He throws his hand up to shield his face from her and averts his eyes. "I'm an angel sent from your risen Lord with a message for you. He's telling me to remind you that Jesus ministered to whores and lepers and the unclean." Looming over him, she finishes. "How dare you place your authority above his."

"I understand." He waves her away with both hands. "Please, just leave me."

Victoria buttons her blouse. "I'll leave you now. But I am going to stick around, just to make sure you do the right thing."

"Yes, yes. I will. Please just go."

Later that afternoon, Davide knocks on the door of Victoria's room and steps in.

"Victoria, I have the most wonderful news. I just spoke to Father Barone, and he says he has reconsidered. He will allow Gisele to be buried with our parents."

"Did he say why?"

"He mentioned something about a vision that reminded him that his authority was not greater than that of the Lord's, but he did not explain what he meant by that."

"Must be a sign from above."

When Victoria returns home following Gisele's funeral she spends more than a month in her room, hardly eating, just sitting in bed staring at the wall. She refuses to see anyone other than Mrs. Mayfair, who spends her time with Victoria consoling her. The household staff worries about her, including Giles, who's never had much use for Victoria.

At last, Victoria asks Mrs. Mayfair to inform Bergeron that she'll dine with him that evening. Nearing the dining room, she sees Giles, who nods in his usual officious manner as she approaches but then gives her a sympathetic smile.

"It's good to have you back, ma'am."

She squeezes his hand. "Thank you, Mr. Giles."

Bergeron is seated when she enters. He rises but does not approach her.

"So glad to have you back among the living."

She lets the comment pass and sits at the opposite end of the table.

Bergeron sits and continues his oration. "I know you've been through a rough situation, but it's something you'll have to learn. We go on, they don't." He leans toward her. "Just as I said, you always lose them."

Victoria looks at him and though her lower lip is quivering, she manages to smile.

"You're wrong, Bergeron. I haven't lost her." She places her hand on her heart. "She's right here." A tear runs down her cheek. "And she'll be there for as long as I live."

The next day Victoria calls on Renee at the Fox's London home where Renee greets her then gives her a long hug. "Are you all right?"

"No, but I'll manage."

"What can I do for you?"

"I hear you're looking for an accompanist."

THIS TOO SHALL PASS

With his wife Anne's death in 1890, Cedric Stepney suddenly feels the weight of the years on him. His own health has been declining the past few decades, but he has remained vigorous enough to make it to the shop and carry out his duties. Now that Anne is gone, and despite having Allison around to encourage him, he no longer feels the same drive to keep going that he did while Anne was still with him.

For the past few years, Allison has been taking over the managerial responsibilities of the business, but she's nowhere near the tailor her father is. Even with his failing eyesight and difficulty using the needle and thread, he has an instinctive ability that Allison lacks. Not willing to let the shop close without Cedric, Allison begins searching for a new person who can take over the responsibilities.

Several weeks after the inquiry is posted, a young man wearing a dark suit and a grey cap enters the shop and removes his cap. He appears to be in his twenties and is of average height with a small frame. When he removes his cap, his dark hair falls into his eyes, but he brushes it back with his hand. Allison is working behind the counter and looks up.

"May I help you, sir?"

"Quite the contrary, ma'am. I believe I can help you."

Allison considers this. "You're here about the position."

"That's right, ma'am. Might you be Miss Stepney?"

"I might be." Allison steps from behind the counter and offers her hand.

"I'm Jeffery Bowman, ma'am. I believe I have just the skills you're looking for."

"Where have you apprenticed?"

"I learned the trade at my uncle's knee. Milton Crossley, who had a shop over on Saville Row."

"He had a good reputation. Didn't he pass away recently?"

"He did, ma'am, and I'd have been happy to take over his business, but his wife was asking too much and wasn't willing to let me work it off."

"That's too bad. Wait here, I'll get my father."

She brings Cedric out and introduces Jeffery. When he hears the name of Jeffery's uncle, he roars with laughter.

"Old Milt. If you learned from him, you can't be all that bad."

"He taught me everything he knew."

"Come on back to the office young man, let's get acquainted."

Allison locks the door and puts out the Back in 30 Minutes sign then follows them back.

Cedric and Allison describe the job and what they'll expect from Jeffery.

"I believe I am capable of meeting all your expectations and am looking forward to joining you if you feel I'm worthy."

"You're acceptable to me, young man. If Allison's in agreement, you can start working with me on some projects, just to get your feet wet."

Allison stares at Jeffery for a moment. "No."

Cedric and Jeffery look at one another, then at Allison.

"Allie, what are you saying?"

Allison disappears into the work room then returns with an envelope full of papers and hands it to Jeffery.

"This is an order for Judge Alexander of the Old Bailey. He's getting a new suit coat with two pairs of trousers. It needs to be ready for a fitting tomorrow at four."

Cedric looks from Jeffery to Allison. "Allie, are you sure about this? Judge Alexander is one of our oldest clients."

"Absolutely. Mr. Bowman says he has the experience. Let's find out."

Jeffery takes some pages from the envelope and looks over them.

"Looks like I have some work to do. I like a challenge."

Allison steps back and motions toward the room she just exited. "The workroom's over here. If there's something you need that's not there, let us know."

Jeffery stands, nods to Allison and Cedric. "Very good, ma'am."

He exits into the workroom.

"Allie, this is very risky." Cedric speaks in a confidential tone. "We don't know how this young man will fare."

"Which is precisely why I want him to handle this job. If he can satisfy our oldest and most demanding client with just a day and a half to work then there's nothing else he'll encounter here that will be worse."

Cedric smiles then nods and points at Allison.

"I like how you think. Sink or swim."

"Besides, if the judge isn't happy, it's doubtful he'll go someplace else. We'll apologize and agree to get him something more to his specifications the following day."

Cedric hugs her. "I never should have doubted you."

The following day, when the judge arrives, Cedric shows him to the fitting room. They try on the various components while Cedric makes notes for alterations.

Looking at himself in the mirror, the judge is impressed. "Stepney, once again you've exceeded yourself."

"I'd like to take credit for the work, but it was all performed by our new associate, Jeffery Bowman." Cedric motions for Jeffery to come over then presents him to the judge.

"Well young man, you do excellent work." The judge shakes his hand. "The quality is what I've come to expect from Stepney."

"Thank you, sir."

Once the judge has gone, Allison joins Cedric and Jeffery in the back.

"Mr. Bowman, you've proven yourself admirably."

"Thank you Miss Stepney. I hope I'll continue to do so for many years to come."

Since early 1901, Victoria has been offering piano lessons to any child who can afford the four pence per month she requires. One afternoon she finds herself joined by a young girl who appears to be ten or twelve.

"Afternoon, ma'am, I'm Lainie Robinson. Are you Miss Seely?"

"That's me. What can I do for you, Lainie?"

"I'd like to talk to you about piano lessons. I've always

wanted to learn, and I've been told you're a good teacher."

"Thank you. You know the cost is four pence a month, correct?"

Lainie looks down and digs at the pavement with the toe of her shoe.

"I was sort of hoping you'd take me without payment. My father can't afford it. He'd like me to learn, but he's got other commitments that come first."

"What about your mother?"

"My mum died when I was a small child. I never really knew her."

Victoria puts her hands on her hips. "I'm sorry, but I must stand firm on the cost."

"Yes ma'am."

Victoria leans forward and places her hand on Lainie's shoulder. "The money isn't an issue, Lainie, it's the commitment. I can easily afford to teach you for nothing, but I must have some sign that you'll stay and take the lessons seriously. A commitment of four pence isn't that great but it demonstrates your willingness to make the commitment." She leans in and whispers. "And if you stick with your lessons for a year, you get a full refund."

She winks at Lainie who laughs.

"I understand, ma'am. In fact, I believe I might know a way to earn the cost myself."

"Now I don't want you to do just anything for the money."

"Not to worry ma'am. I know the value of a good day's work."

"Good for you, Lainie." She removes a card from her handbag. "Have you been to school?"

"I have, ma'am. I can read, write, and do math."

"Good." Victoria hands her a card. "When you have the tuition, that's where you can find me."

"Thanks Miss Seely."

Allison is in the back of the shop when she hears Jeffery speaking to someone.

"You're not supposed to be in here."

She hears a child's voice and steps through the curtain to see Jeffery hustling a little girl toward the door.

"Jeffery, what's going on?"

He turns, but before he can speak, the girl steps forward.

"Afternoon, ma'am. My name's Lainie Robinson."

"Good afternoon, Lainie Robinson. I'm Allison Stepney. What can I do for you?"

"I was hoping you might have some jobs you need done. Like stacking boxes or posting letters. I'm quick and will work hard for you."

"Why do you need the job?"

Lainie kicks at the floor and looks down. "Piano lessons, ma'am."

"Piano lessons?"

"Yes, ma'am. I'd like to study piano with Miss Seely, and it costs four pence a month. My father can't afford it because times have been awfully hard, and I thought I could try to make the money myself."

"Couldn't Miss Seely bend a bit on the cost?"

"She doesn't need the money, but she says that by paying the fee, I'll be demonstrating my commitment to the lessons." She motions for Allison to lean down and when she does, Lainie whispers to her, "And she said she'd refund the cost if I'm still with her in a year."

"Well, Lainie, I think we may be able to find something for you around the shop."

Allison looks over at Jeffery who gives her a resigned shrug.

Lainie brightens. "Really?"

"Really. Report back here tomorrow afternoon."

"Yes, ma'am." Lainie hurries to the door but turns before exiting. 'You know, ma'am, now that I think about it, you sort of remind me of Miss Seely."

Allison winks at Lainie. "I'm not sure that's such a good thing for Miss Seely."

Once Lainie leaves, Allison turns to Jeffery.

"You never go wrong by helping someone, Jeffery."

"Yes, ma'am."

Billy Seely walks through the park he's visited every weekend for the past thirty or more years and at irregular intervals for years prior. In earlier times, he'd have been accompanied by his wife Bess or his sons Donald and Willem, but Bess died two months past, and his sons now have wives and families of their own. So, Billy comes to the park alone, to sit on a bench, maybe doze a while. Sometimes one of his buddies happens by and they exchange pleasantries or talk about old times. Many days, he's just there alone. Today is no exception. As he putters along one of the paths, he is reminded of his childhood, when he and his sisters played in the park. Whenever he thinks about those times, he can't help but recall Vickie and wonder what became of her.

Despite the stigma society attached to the illegitimacy of his sisters, Billy never thought less of them. When his mother sent Vickie and Mandy off to the orphanage, Billy made the effort to stay in contact. As they got older, Billy took it upon himself to keep the evil elements of their world away from them. After Amanda was sent down, he tried to make Vickie his chief priority but after he married Bess, she and their boys became his main concern and visits with his sister became less frequent. Even when he learned Vickie had taken to selling herself in Whitechapel he tried to look out for her, until Bess had enough and demanded that he sever ties with his wayward sister.

He recalls with shame the next to last meeting they had. Vickie had gotten into some sort of trouble and needed a few shillings to make her rent. She'd sought out Billy at his home which angered Bess beyond words.

"I don't want her coming by here Billy. You need to get rid of her and tell her not to come back."

When Vickie showed up at his door, Billy took her by the arm and hustled her out the door, shoving her off the front stoop.

Behind him, Bess called out angrily after her, "And stay away from our family you filthy whore!"

The words cut through Billy as he recalls them just as they had when he heard them all those years ago. He was so broken up over it that he went out that evening and sought out Vickie in Whitechapel. Catching sight of her, he ducked into a doorway and as she passed, he called out her name. When she turned he motioned for her to join him, which she did.

"Billy, what are you doing here? I thought your wife said it all at your place earlier."

"Vickie, I'm so sorry about that, but Bess don't want you near the boys or me. I want to help you, but she's my wife."

A tear ran down Vickie's cheek.

"You know I'd never do anything to hurt you. I wouldn't have come to see you at all except that I had nowhere else to turn."

Billy took her hand and placed a pound note into it.

"I hope this does the trick, but you can't come around asking for anything more. I've got to think of my family."

She spoke softly, almost imperceptively. "I'm your family too."

"I know." He placed his hand gently against her cheek. "This is tearing me apart, Vickie."

Checking to be sure they were alone, he stepped out of the doorway, then turned back. "Take care, Vickie. And please watch out. It's dangerous out here."

He hustled off. It was the last time he saw her.

The memories subside as Billy dozes on his bench again. His nap is interrupted by the sound of a familiar voice.

"Morning, Billy."

He opens his eyes and jumps when he sees Vickie standing there, looking no older than she did the last time he saw her, though that had to have been twenty-five years before.

"What? Forgive me, ma'am but you look just like my sister Vickie."

"It's me, Billy."

She sits beside him.

"Vickie? How can this be? You're only a few years younger than I am but you don't look like you've aged a day."

"I'm still getting used to it myself."

A tear rolls down his cheek as he looks away.

"You're a specter, my sister's ghost come to haunt me because I abandoned her."

"I'm not a ghost." She takes his hand and holds it against her cheek then clasps it with both hands in her lap. "See, flesh and blood just like you."

"I don't understand. If you are Vickie, I don't see why you'd want to have anything to do with me, given how horrible I treated you that last time."

"That's in the past. I know you did it for your wife and sons. I never blamed you for any of that. I had my share of problems and shouldn't have brought them to your doorstep."

"Did you know my Bessie's gone?" A tear runs down his cheek. "Thirty years together and now she's gone. I've been out of my head these past few weeks. Don't know how I'll get along."

"You're not alone. I'm here for you."

"That was you. At the graveyard I saw you standing away from everyone and thought I was just imagining it."

"I was there. How are your boys?"

Billy beams with pride. "Donny's got a wife and four children, two boys and two girls with one on the way and Willie's got a wife and little twin girls. They're both working on the docks, making a good wage. They've made me proud."

"That's wonderful."

"But how are you getting along? I hope you're not still—"

"No, I put that behind me a few years ago. There's this gentleman who's given me a room in his place for several years and he's been teaching me. I've learned how to read and write, how to speak French and Italian. Billy, I've learned to play the piano. I'm making a living at that."

"That's good to hear. You were always good with music. But what do you do for this man? He's just letting you stay there?"

Vickie looks away, considering something.

"Billy, there's something I've got to tell you, something I've learned about myself. It's going to sound impossible, so I'll understand if you don't believe me."

Billy takes her hands in his. "What is it? You can tell me anything, Vickie."

"This gentleman tells me I'm not aging like everyone else does, and because of it, I'm going to look young for many years. Hundreds even. And that I'm going to be alive for a thousand or more years."

"Blimey. It sounds like crazy talk, but, looking at you, it's hard not to believe. I remember when you were twenty and you don't look much older now."

"This gentleman is like that as well. Only he's been around for a lot longer. When he met me and found out I was like him he asked me to come live at his place so he'd have someone around he knew would live as long as him. He's not asking for anything more than my company. We just sit and talk, and he teaches me about the world."

"Sounds like a good deal." He puts his arm around her and pulls her to him. "Oh, Vickie, it's so good to see you again. I'm glad to hear you're okay. This gift you've been given is wonderful. I hope you use it to really make something of yourself."

"I plan to try."

After reconciling with Billy, Victoria makes a point to meet him in the park each weekend. Sometimes they talk about their past, or catch one another up on current events, or speculate on what Amanda is doing now. One Saturday, he isn't there and Victoria inquires at his home to find out he has been taken ill. Learning that his sons and their families are due that evening, Vickie arranges a visit with Billy a few hours before. It's obvious when she sees him that he won't last much longer.

Billy reaches out to her. "Vickie. You've come. I'm so glad you made it."

"I'm always here for you, Billy." She puts her arms around him and stays with him for over an hour, chatting until he drops off to sleep. Then she kisses him on the forehead.

"Goodbye, Billy."

On her way out, a tall, muscular man whose face is the very image of Billy's, is about to enter, but pauses to hold the door for her. "Ev'ning ma'am. Have you been in with my father?"

"Yes. My name's Elizabeth Mayfair. My family knew him in Whitechapel some years back and I wanted to drop in and pay my respects when I heard he was ill."

"Bless you, ma'am. I'm Donald, his eldest son."

"It's good to meet you, Donald. He's a good man, your father."

Victoria leaves him and though she feels tears coming on, she holds herself together until she gets around the corner. Then she collapses against the wall of a building, puts her hands over her face and breaks down into heavy sobs. It is the first time she has ever met or spoken with either of her nephews.

Two days later, Vickie receives word that Billy has died. She spends the evening in her room being comforted by Mrs. Mayfair. She wishes she could write to Amanda in Australia, but Amanda stopped writing after only a few letters and never let them know where she settled after her sentence was lifted. Victoria lowers her head onto Mrs. Mayfair's lap and sobs uncontrollably. She feels completely alone.

Several blocks away from Bergeron's residence, Allison Stepney is preparing to close Stepney & Sons for the evening, when a lanky man with an unruly mop of brown hair enters the shop.

"Ev'ning ma'am." The man removes his cap. "Hope I'm not too late."

"Not at all. How may I help you?"

"My name's Willem Seely, ma'am, and I'd like to look into getting a suit."

"Certainly, sir. Is this for a particular occasion?"

"Yes ma'am, my father's funeral."

Allison bows her head slightly. "My sympathies to your family."

"Thank you, ma'am. I've got a suit I wore when my

Mom died, but it's getting somewhat worn in places, and I'm to be one of the pallbearers this time, so I think I should try to look my best."

"Right this way. We'll get some measurements and I'll show you some styles." She leads him into the fitting room. "Seely. I've heard that name. Tell me about your father."

Brigitte strolls down the sidewalk, gazing in shop windows without really intending to purchase anything. She's in London for a performance at Covent Gardens, but she's beginning to tire of life on the road, living out of suitcases. She wants to travel without the added burden of having to perform, or drag along some amorous male cohort, to see the world in ways other than from a stage, and to make the most out of the fact that she'll be alive for a very long time.

She suddenly recalls that the director of the company is leaving, and she has been charged with getting him a suitable present to commemorate his years of service. Across the street, she spies a familiar sign, Stepney & Sons, and she recalls visiting it fifteen or twenty years prior with a male companion who was also in need of the perfect accessory. She enters the shop and is greeted by a young man behind one of the counters.

"I'm looking for a set of cufflinks. I recall an acquaintance of mine purchased a set of diamond studded cufflinks here some years ago." She reflects on this. "And another set the following day I believe."

"I don't recall the set. Let me fetch the proprietor and maybe she'll remember them."

Brigitte chuckles at the irony inherent in a shop called Stepney & Sons being run by a woman. A sound from behind her causes her to turn. A thin, awkward-looking woman, with strawberry blond hair pulled back away from her face, is standing in the doorway leading into the back of the shop. Brigitte recalls speaking to the woman in French when she was in the shop before, and the woman hasn't changed at all.

When she first sees Brigitte, she seems startled, but says nothing about it and recovers quickly.

"Jeffery said you were looking for cufflinks." There's a note of discomfort in her voice.

"Yes." Brigitte cannot pull her eyes away from the woman who becomes self-conscious and looks away. She motions toward the far counter.

"We have a quite a good selection over here."

Brigitte follows her over to the counter and she recalls the woman's name from their previous conversation.

"Votre nom est Allison n'est pas lui?"

Allison looks frightened for a moment but covers with a nervous chuckle. "Yes, ma'am. Have you been here before?"

"Il y a quinze ou vingt ans. Je vous note pour ne pas avoir changé beaucoup."

Allison looks at her nervously.

Brigitte reverts to English. "I'm curious. When were you born?"

"Why would you want to know something like that, ma'am?"

"I'm just interested in how old you are. Perhaps we are the same age."

Allison stares at her for a long time. "Jeffery?"

"Yes, ma'am."

"Why don't you take your lunch now?"

"Certainly, ma'am."

She follows him to the door, where he turns. "By the way, ma'am, I have an engagement this afternoon that will require me being out of the shop. I've asked my brother to fill in for me if that's all right. We don't have any clients due, and he's worked in similar shops before."

"Yes, that's fine." She closes then locks the door and puts out the Back in 30 Minutes sign. Marching over to Brigitte, she grabs her by the arm and pulls her into the back room.

"Why are you asking me all these questions? What business is it of yours when I was born?"

"I'm just curious. I remember you from all those years ago and you don't seem to have aged since then."

"That's ridiculous. Everyone ages."

"I don't. At least not like everyone else."

This leaves Allison speechless as the words sink in.

"When were you born?"

"1786."

"1786?"

"Of course. In Paris before poor Louis lost his head. And you?"

Allison looks down and crosses her arms.

"I don't know when I was born exactly. My parents said they found me dead on a trash heap, but God brought me back to life. This was in 1848 and they said I looked like I was just a few weeks old, so it had to have been around that time. I've looked like this since the late-60s."

Brigitte nods. "Yes, I've heard we can rise from the dead as well."

"Why are we like this?"

"Who can say? I just accept that it's how I am and try to enjoy it."

Allison sits down. "I wish I could enjoy it. All the people I knew when I was a child are getting old. They think I'm some sort of freak. I never used to hear their comments when my parents were still around, but now that they're gone, I hear people all the time saying how unnatural I am. I suppose I could spend time with younger people, but I don't understand any of the new trends or how to keep up, so I don't fit into that crowd either."

Brigitte has been admiring the drawings on the wall.

"Did you do these?"

"Yes I did." Allison joins her and points to the ones she has on the wall. "These are ones I did 'round town." Then she indicates the ones on the counter "And these are some of my fashion drawings."

"You are very talented." Brigitte turns to Allison. "I'm going to be in a show tonight at Covent Gardens. Would you like to attend? You could be my guest."

"Could I?"

"Of course. And afterward you can join me and my friends at a party."

"I'd like that. Are any of them—?"

"No. But they're a lot of fun to be around. When your man comes back, why don't you take the remainder of the day off and I'll help you find the perfect dress for the party."

"All right," Allison says excitedly.

Brigitte smiles and says, "And now, about those cufflinks."

Allison holds up her finger and motions toward the showroom. "I believe I recall just the pair you mean."

Victoria has been teaching Lainie for several months and on numerous occasions Lainie has mentioned Allison Stepney and how much she resembles Victoria. Finally, Victoria decides to see for herself. Following directions given her by Lainie, Victoria spots the sign for Stepney & Sons, crosses the street, and enters.

"Yes ma'am," the young man behind the counter says.

"I'm looking for Miss Stepney. I'm Victoria Seely."

"Miss Stepney is out for the afternoon."

"Do you expect her back this evening?"

"To be honest ma'am, I can't say. I'm filling in for my brother Jeffery who also had an engagement this afternoon. My understanding, though, is that Miss Stepney is out for the remainder of the day, though whether she plans to look in at any point, I couldn't tell you."

"I see." She takes a card from her purse and hands it to him. "Please tell her Victoria Seely called and I'll try to look in on her later if I get a chance."

"Might I mention what this is in regard to?"

"A mutual friend."

Once Jeffery returns from lunch, Allison informs him she'll be running errands the remainder of the day. Brigitte takes her to all the best clothing stores searching for the perfect party gown. They decide on an off-the-shoulder emerald-green dress with gold accents, matching shoes, white gloves, and a nice hat to go with it.

Brigette examines her, wearing a wide smile. "Quite a change, no?"

"Is it really me?"

"We're not quite done yet."

Brigette takes Allison by the theater and introduces her to the woman who does the hair and makeup for the performers. Allison leaves with a new hair style to go with her new clothes. She changes in Brigitte's room, and they board a carriage for the theater.

At the party, Allison is both fascinated and a bit anxious being around all Brigitte's theatrical friends and Brigitte seems to sense this.

"Here. Let me introduce you to the company director and some of the dancers."

She leads Allison over to a small group gathered around a trim, clean-shaven man.

"This is my friend Allison. Please make her feel welcome."

"Do you perform?" the director asks.

"Oh no. I'm proprietor of a tailoring shop."

One of the dancers says, "Perhaps I should pay you a visit. I'm in need of a new suit."

"Certainly. I'll tell you how to find us before the evening is over."

Whenever Allison reconnects with Brigitte, she encourages Allison to approach someone or gives her tips on what to talk about before introducing her to someone else.

"You should tell them you're a designer. Our company always has a need for someone to create costumes for us."

"I don't think I have enough experience."

"You never know. Besides, you have to start somewhere."

At one point, Allison notices a dapper man in a tuxedo with a close-cropped beard and a walking stick who has been eyeing them for several minutes.

"Brigitte, that man's looking at us."

"Au contraire. I believe he is looking at you."

"What should I do?"

"You could speak to him."

"But what should I say?"

"You could try hello."

"Do you know him?"

"Yes, that's Jean-Paul. Go talk to him."

Saying this, she shoos Allison away. Allison nervously approaches Jean-Paul and nods. "Hello."

"Good evening, madam. I saw you speaking to Brigitte and did not wish to intrude."

"Oh, that's all right. We're just— chatting."

"I thought I knew all of Brigitte's friends, but I don't recognize you. I am Jean-Paul."

"I'm Allison." She extends her hand. He takes it and kisses it. She blushes.

"And what does Allison do when you aren't attending these functions with Brigitte?"

They speak for several minutes alternating between French and English then Allison returns to Brigitte.

"He's asked me to have a drink with him elsewhere."

"Ah, that's a very good sign. He will most likely invite you to his suite before the evening is over."

"Is that good?"

"That depends on your perspective, but I know Jean-Paul and if you lack experience, he is the perfect person to be with. He's young but he thinks like a much older man. He's very gentle and patient and won't ask you to do anything you do not wish to do. It should be very— pleasurable?"

Brigitte smiles as suddenly Allison realizes what she's talking about, blushes, then giggles, covering her mouth. Jean-Paul approaches.

"Brigitte, I hope your friend is not telling you what a bore I am."

"Oh, you're not a bore. I was just telling her we're headed off for some drinks."

Jean-Paul offers her his arm, she takes it and as they walk away, she looks over her shoulder at Brigitte who winks.

The next morning, Brigitte calls for Allison at Stepney & Sons, but the clerk tells her Allison hasn't arrived yet. As she's leaving, she spots Allison strolling along the street, wearing the same clothes she had on the previous evening. She's humming.

"Well, I suppose I don't have to ask you how things went."

Allison says nothing, but as she passes, she gives Brigitte a satisfied smile over her shoulder then winks. "Un marveilleux temps a été eu par tous."

As Allison enters, Brigitte can hear the young man behind the counter exclaim, "Miss Stepney?"

Victoria listens as Lainie Robinson finishes her lesson for that day. At the conclusion, Victoria claps and gives Lainie a quick hug. "Very good. You've made a lot of progress."

She walks with Lainie out to the street with her hand resting on Lainie's shoulder.

"Same time next week, okay?"

"Yes ma'am. Do you think I'm ready for the Chopin piece, ma'am?"

Victoria processes this thought, tilting her head from right to left.

"We can try it. See how you do, okay?"

"Certainly! Thank you ma'am!"

Victoria stops Lainie as she turns to leave. "Oh wait. I almost forgot I have a present for you."

"A present for me?"

Victoria removes a small box from her handbag. "It's for being a good student." She opens the box and removes a silver chain with a charm in the shape of a musical note.

"It's lovely." Lainie admires the charm as she holds it in the palm of her hand. Victoria motions for her to turn around and she places the chain around her neck and fastens it.

"Now if your father says anything, tell him it wasn't expensive at all. Just say it's a reward for being such an excellent student."

"Yes ma'am." Lainie darts across the street then waves. "I'm never taking it off."

Victoria watches Lainie move away. When she turns back toward the house, she thinks she catches sight of Bergeron at the window of his study with the curtains slightly parted. When she looks closer, though, he's not there. She decides she must have imagined it.

Allison and Jeffery are in the front of the shop when a young man enters.

"I'm Tommy Robinson. Lainie's brother."

Allison comes from behind the counter and approaches him. "Good to meet you, Tommy. Lainie's not here right now but she may be this afternoon."

Tommy lowers his head.

"I didn't think she'd be here, but I thought I'd give it a try all the same. Lainie didn't come home last night and we're all terribly worried about her."

Allison gives Jeffery a look of concern then puts her hand on Tommy's shoulder. "Could she have gone off with a friend?"

"I doubt that ma'am. It's not like her to just run off like this. She usually lets our father know where she'll be."

"I haven't seen her for a few days." Allison looks to Jeffery. "Was she here yesterday?"

"No ma'am. She looked in around three-o-clock the previous day, but we didn't have any jobs for her at that time."

Allison nods and faces Tommy again. "You tell your father if there's anything we can do, to let us know. Lainie's a good girl and we'll do whatever we can to see that she returns home safely."

"Yes, ma'am. Thank you, ma'am."

He leaves.

"That's perfectly dreadful." Allison steps behind the counter again. "I can't imagine what they must be going through."

Jeffery shakes his head. "I'll be sure to remember them in my prayers this evening."

A day passes without news. The following day, Allison returns from an errand to find Jeffery leaning on the counter, very upset.

"What's wrong?"

"They found Lainie, ma'am." His voice is shaky. "Her

brother came by—"

"Please tell me she's all right."

In response, Jeffery can only shake his head. Allison covers her mouth and looks down, tears in her eyes. Several long moments pass before she regains her voice.

"Did he say what happened?"

"Someone murdered her." Jeffery's tone is a mixture of sorrow and anger. "That dear little girl. They found her in an alley. Police suspect she was strangled then her throat was cut."

"My god. What sort of monster could harm a sweet child like that?"

"I'm not certain I want to know the answer to that."

Allison dabs at her eyes with her handkerchief.

"Is the family receiving visitors currently?"

"I don't know. I suppose it wouldn't hurt to check."

They close the shop and head over to where Lainie told them she lived. They find a group of neighbors gathered around the front door. Allison introduces herself and Jeffery and they are admitted to the residence. A tall young man with sandy-colored hair greets them inside.

"Miss Stepney, Mr. Bowman. Lainie has always had the best things to say about you. I'm her brother, Bernard. She was truly grateful for the job in your shop."

Allison takes his hands. "Is your father at home?"

Bernard looks down. "He is, ma'am, but he's not able to have guests at present. This has taken all the life out of him. Lainie was his special child. She was special to all of us. I don't know how we'll go on without her."

Jeffery grasps his shoulder. "Somehow you'll find the strength. If for no other reason than to keep alive her memory."

Bernard nods. "You're right, Mr. Bowman. If nothing else, we should go on for her."

"Please tell your father that if there's anything he or your family needs, he only has to ask," Allison says. "Lainie was special to us as well."

"Bless you, ma'am."

As they head back to the shop, Allison takes out her handkerchief. "As long as I live I will never understand how someone could be so cruel. I doubt Lainie ever hurt a single person. How someone could do something so horrible—"

Her voice breaks and she can't continue. Jeffery puts his arm around her and rubs her back.

"Perhaps it's not for us to understand, but just to be happy that we had the opportunity to know her while she was here."

On Thursday, Lainie doesn't show up for her weekly piano lesson. Forty-five minutes later, Stewart Crandall, Victoria's last student of the day, arrives ahead of schedule.

"Stew, you're in luck. Lainie didn't show up so I can take you early."

Stewart seems surprised. "Ma'am, I thought you'd have heard. Lainie's dead."

"What?" Victoria falls back against the doorframe, her hand over her mouth. "What happened?"

"She was found murdered in an alley. I live one street over from her family and they was out looking for her after she didn't come home one afternoon. Police found her body a few nights ago."

Tears are rolling down Victoria's cheeks and she rocks back and forth against the door frame. She dabs at her eyes with a handkerchief.

"That beautiful girl. Her family must be devastated." She places her hand on Stew's shoulder. "After our lesson, will you walk me over to the family's home? I'd like to pay my respects."

At the family's residence, Victoria is greeted at the door by Lainie's father. She introduces herself.

"Miss Seely, Lainie always spoke so highly of you. She enjoyed her lessons, looked forward to 'em every week. When she came back last time she was so excited that she was going to start learning a new piece."

"She was a joy to work with." Victoria clasps his hands. "And very talented. You must be very proud of her."

"We were, ma'am."

Victoria leans in and speaks in a low voice. "Stewart Crandall told me what happened. I'll understand if you don't want to talk about it, but it's just so hard to believe."

"I know, ma'am. They found her in an alley not far from here. The police say she was strangled then her throat was cut."

Victoria places her hand on her throat.

"Who could do such a terrible thing to such a sweet little girl?" Robinson begins to cry. "It made me think back to the Ripper, but that was so long ago, it couldn't be could it?"

Robinson breaks down and Victoria puts her arms around him consoling him. "Let's hope not."

When Victoria arrives back at the house, Mrs. Mayfair is waiting outside Victoria's room. She stops long enough to hand Mrs. Mayfair her hat and handbag then starts up toward Bergeron's study.

"Will you be wanting some dinner?"

"Not now!"

As she climbs the last few steps, she can hear Bergeron moving around in the study. He's whistling a tune and Victoria recognizes as an excerpt from the Chopin piece she was going to have Lainie start on that day. She storms through the door and slams it hard behind her.

"Victoria. You seem a little out of sorts. Have some sherry."

"You lying, murdering, bastard! You killed that little girl, didn't you?"

"Someone's been killed?"

"Yes, a beautiful, talented girl who had so much promise. What was it? You couldn't be such a person yourself, so you had to destroy someone who was?"

"Victoria, you're overreacting. Do you even have any proof I was involved."

"I have proof all right." She touches her neck. "I'll carry it with me 'til the day I die."

"Oh, there you go dredging up the past again. I thought we were beyond that."

"How could I ever be beyond it?" Victoria circles and moves closer to Bergeron.

"So, Whitechapel has one less dirty little street urchin running around. The surplus population could use a little trimming."

"Don't you dare trivialize this. That little girl trusted me. She wasn't expecting to have her throat cut."

Bergeron laughs. "She was trusting wasn't she?"

He alternates between an exaggerated cockney accent in a childish voice and his own.

"I could tell you where that shop is, sir. Matter of fact, I could take you there."

"What a smart girl you are. You show me the way and I'll give you a pound note."

"Right this way sir."

"So, trusting, and so giving." Saying this he opens three fingers on his clenched hand, allowing a silver chain to fall, dangling from his thumb and forefinger. At the end is a charm in the shape of a musical note.

Victoria angrily rushes toward him, grabbing for the chain. "Give that to me!"

Bergeron snatches it away and grabs her by the arms then slams her against the wall, knocking the wind out of her. He places his hand to her throat but does not apply any pressure.

"She never saw it coming. So eager to please. Sound like someone else? Maybe fourteen years ago?" He releases her and sits at his desk, folds his hands in front of him. "She was a fighter, too, arms and legs flailing, jerking at the cord. I was afraid I'd get caught. So much life. So easily snuffed."

Victoria wipes the tears away and speaks in an angry whisper. "She was twelve years old."

He slams his fist onto the desk. "What's that to me? Twelve, twenty-four, fifty, it's all the same."

"I ought to turn you in to the police right now."

"And what exactly will you tell them?" He once again adopts a cockney accent. "Please sirs, I was killed by this man fourteen years ago, but I came back to life. Now he's gone and killed another girl. Please arrest him."

Victoria looks away from him and down. "She's not the only one, is she?" She moves to the edge of the desk. "I recall there being some murders in Paris when we were there. I didn't think much of it at the time, but now I've got to wonder if you were behind those." She turns, walks a few steps away then turns back. "All these years, I've wanted to believe you'd changed. I let my guard down. But you'll never change, will you?"

Bergeron stands and walks to Victoria, circling her.

"You lived in my house, accepted my hospitality, allowed me to take you to concerts, plays, operas, ballets. You've eaten my food, made use of my servants, never once objected when I footed the bill for your clothes, your language or music lessons. I let you bring your French whore over whenever you wanted without so much as raising an eyebrow. I would have killed her, but she beat me to it. You're nothing more than the same piece of trash I plucked out of the garbage of Whitechapel fourteen years ago. I want you out of my house, out of my sight, out of my life. I'll give you one week."

Victoria meets his eyes. "I don't need a week."

She hurries out of the study and down the stairs, nearly tripping. At her door, she grabs Mrs. Mayfair and pushes her inside.

"Do you have somewhere you can stay tonight? Other than here."

"What do you mean?"

"Just answer me!" Victoria gives her a fearful look.

Mrs. Mayfair shakes her head and thinks it over. "My brother, I suppose, but why would I want to do that?"

Victoria ignores the question. "Let's go to your room. I'll help you pack whatever you need for overnight then go to your brothers. Get Giles to walk with you, though. Do not go alone."

Mrs. Mayfair puts her hands up. "Victoria, you're not making any sense."

"I just had it out with Bergeron. I found out he's been lying about a lot of things and confronted him about it. He told me to get out within the week, but I'm not waiting that long. You need to come with me, but for tonight you cannot remain under his roof."

"Don't be silly. Mr. Bergeron wouldn't hurt me."

Victoria suddenly recalls the odd conversation she had with the mysterious woman right after she came to live at Bergeron's. She grabs Mrs. Mayfair and stares into her eyes. "It's not you he wants to hurt."

Mrs. Mayfair considers this a moment. "Let's go get my things."

Once Mrs. Mayfair has gone, Victoria hurries back to her room, locks the door then props a chair under the knob for added security. She begins packing as much as she can into several trunks which she slides to beside the door. Finished with the larger items, she surveys the room then finishes packing a small suitcase and sets it by the door for the servants to take out. Finally, she lies on the bed, still fully dressed, and takes from under the mattress a large carving knife she bought a few days after moving into the house. She slips it under a pillow then lies back so she can keep an eye on the door then falls into an uneasy sleep.

When she awakens a few hours later, it is still dark. She lies in bed until she hears the chiming of Big Ben, signaling five-o-clock. She sits up and fetches a piece of hard candy from her side table to help stop the rumbling in her stomach. Mrs. Mayfair is due back just after sunrise and is ordering a carriage. Victoria sits up in bed and closes her eyes, listening for any indication that Bergeron is in the house, but she hears nothing. She lies back on her side then feels for the knife under her pillow. Finding it still there, she allows herself to drift off into sleep again.

The next thing she's aware of is the sound of someone tapping on her door.

"Who is it?"

"It's Polly from downstairs, ma'am. I couldn't find Liz Mayfair and was wondering if you wanted some breakfast."

"Thank you. I'll be down shortly."

"Yes ma'am."

Victoria looks out the window to see the sun just appearing over the tops of nearby buildings, so she removes the chair from her door. She plans to meet Mrs. Mayfair the minute she arrives.

Victoria takes her purse, descends the stairs, and steps out onto the front steps. There she spots Giles leaning against the wall, looking down and shaking his head.

"Mr. Giles are you all right?"

"I'll be fine ma'am. Mr. Bergeron has informed me he no longer requires my services. I'm sure I'll find another situation."

"He let you go?"

"Yes ma'am. He's replacing all the staff I understand. He may even put the house up for sale."

Shaking her head, Victoria reaches into her purse and takes out several bills. She takes his hand and presses the bills into it.

"Oh no, ma'am. I couldn't—"

"You have no choice, Giles, because I'm not taking them back."

"But ma'am, there must be nearly a hundred pounds here."

"It is one hundred pounds. That should help you out until you find another situation." She thinks a moment then removes one of her calling cards and jots the address of Charles and Renee Fox on the back of it. "These people are looking for someone, come to think of it. Have you heard of Charles and Renee?"

"No ma'am."

"Tell them I recommended them to you. That should do it."

"Thank you ma'am, but I don't understand. I was never happy with your being here and I can't recall but a few times I ever had a kind word for you. Most of those were when Mr. Bergeron told me to."

She shrugs.

"Maybe I never gave you any reason to like me." She pats his arm. "You take care of yourself, Mr. Giles."

He bows and tips his hat. "Thank you ma'am, and may God smile upon you all your days."

As she turns from Giles, she sees Mrs. Mayfair approaching, accompanied by a large chubby man with curly hair that's just starting to go gray.

When they get to Victoria, Mrs. Mayfair presents him.

"Victoria Seely, this is my brother, Clayton Wells."

Victoria shakes his hand. "Your family name is Wells. I've always wondered."

"That's right, ma'am. Before she was Elizabeth Mayfair, she was plain ol' Lizzie Wells."

Mrs. Mayfair swats his arm. "You behave yourself around my friends."

Clayton salutes.

The three of them go inside and pack up Mrs. Mayfair's things. Back outside, Clayton salutes again.

"If you ladies will excuse me, I'll be on my way."

Once he's gone, Victoria halts the servant who's carrying her baggage out to the curb. "Arnold, once you have my bags loaded, please help Mrs. Mayfair with hers. The carriage should be arriving shortly."

Once their bags are loaded, Victoria boards the carriage accompanied by Mrs. Mayfair, who's wearing a cape and her best bonnet.

"Ready?" Victoria pats Mrs. Mayfair's hand.

"I am."

Once they're underway, Victoria leans toward her. "Elizabeth, there's something you need to know."

"What's that, dear?"

"I'm not just leaving the house, I'm leaving England. I'm going to America and I'm not coming back. I want you there with me."

"Oh, I don't know. I've never thought of it before." She pats Victoria's hand. "But what is it that's said in the Scriptures, 'whither thou go, I will go'? If you need me, I'll be there."

A few weeks after Lainie's death, Allison runs across Victoria's card at the shop and recalls that she had planned to look in on her. As she's preparing to leave the country in a few days, she decides to drop in that afternoon.

At the address on Victoria's card she's greeted by a servant. "I'm Allison Stepney calling for Miss Seely."

"Miss Seely no longer resides here, ma'am."

"Really? Would you know where I could find her?"

"No ma'am, she left no instructions on where to forward inquiries. Mr. Bergeron, the owner of the house has told us he don't want us spending any time on it."

"Did she leave under difficult circumstances?"

"I can't say, ma'am. Right after she left, Mr. Bergeron sacked the entire staff and hired all new people."

"So, you didn't know Miss Seely?"

"That is correct, ma'am."

"Is Mr. Bergeron at home?"

"No ma'am. He has left the city for an indeterminate time."

She takes out a calling card.

"I wonder if I might leave my card for Mr. Bergeron. If he's back within the next week and could give me any information on how to reach Miss Seely, I would appreciate it."

Allison and Jeffery sit opposite one another in a meeting room at the office of Allison's solicitor, listening as Jeffery's attorney reads from an official document.

"Know all men by these presents, and so on." He skims the document. "Ah, here we are. The conditions of this agreement are as follows. That upon execution, Miss Allison Anne Stepney and Mister Jeffery Walter Bowman shall form a partnership for the purposes of maintaining the business currently known as Stepney & Sons, Fine Menswear. That Miss Stepney and Mister Bowman shall be equal partners in said enterprise. That Mr. Bowman shall assume all managerial responsibilities and shall have authority to make decisions based on his sole discretion, though Miss Stepney may overrule said decisions should she be able to show just cause in doing so, and that the business shall retain the name Stepney & Sons for the remainder of its existence. Signed by our hands and witnessed this fourteenth day of September, one thousand nine hundred and two." He skims it again. "Everything seems to be in order."

Allison's attorney nods. "We'll have you each sign five

copies, one for each of you, one to be retained with each solicitor, and one to be filed in the records office."

He slides copies to each of them. They sign then pass the papers over to the other and sign those copies. When all the paperwork has been handled, Jeffery and Allison shake hands across the table.

"Congratulations, Jeffery. I know you'll continue the fine traditions established at Stepney & Sons."

"Thank you Miss— er, Allison. I don't know what prompted this move, but I appreciate that you have this much confidence in me. I promise I won't let you down."

"I know you won't. I'm sure my father would be proud to have you in charge as well."

As they're leaving, Allison says to her solicitor, "You have my instructions on what to do with the proceeds from the sale of my home, correct?"

He nods. "The local orphans' fund will be appreciative."

As Allison and Jeffery walk to the door, he says, "So you're really leaving England?"

"I certainly am, Jeffery. I'll be in Paris tomorrow and from there, who knows?"

"It won't be the same without you in the shop. I'm not sure how I'll manage."

"You'll do fine. How's your brother working out?"

"He's doing a passable job. In a few days, he'll be fully up to speed."

"Very good."

They reach the street then turn to face one another.

"Will I be seeing you again, Allison?"

"I can't say. I'm sure I'll be back at some point. In the meantime, you take care of yourself, Jeffery. You've always been a good friend."

"And you too, Allison. I don't know what's gotten into you recently, but it's been a pleasure to see. I hope everything turns out well for you."

She leans in, kisses him on the cheek and gives him a quick hug then turns and heads toward her home. Most of her bags are packed and waiting for the carriage to pick them up. She packs a few more items in a handbag then stops to take a last look around at her family's home.

"Mother and Father. Thank you for everything you've done for me. I hope I make you proud."

She heads out just as the carriage pulls up.

The following afternoon, she and Brigitte are sitting at a cafe in Paris having a late lunch.

"If I haven't told you yet, I want to thank you."

"Thank me for what?"

Allison pats Brigitte's hand then grasps it. "All my life my parents told me I was a miracle child, that God had some sort of special plans for me that he'd reveal when he was ready. It was so overwhelming; I never knew quite how to deal with it. But you showed me that I was special in a completely different way and that it doesn't carry any conditions to it."

"Glad I could be of assistance. Why don't we see what the world has in store for the two of us?"

"I'm with you."

Victoria and Mrs. Mayfair are in their temporary lodgings for only a few days before their scheduled departure date for America. The little time they have is spent packing whatever they want to take and divesting themselves of anything they don't want. Victoria also has a few matters to settle with her solicitor.

"Donald and Willem Seely, my nephews, live with their families in the East End. I don't really know them, but I want to look out for them all the same. After I've gone, I want you to prepare two bank drafts in the amount of one thousand pounds each."

"Quite a lot for two fellows you don't know."

"I may not know them, but I knew and loved my brother Billy. I'd like to see that his sons enjoy some financial freedom."

"We'll do as you wish."

"I have no doubt that you will." She writes out the names and addresses of her nephews. "Tell them it's from their aunt, Victoria. Let them know she went to America and made good of herself and in the end, she remembered them in her will."

"Very good, Miss Seely. We'll see that it's done. Will there be anything else?"

"Have you prepared the power of attorney?"

"Yes ma'am." He produces the document. Victoria looks over it and signs.

"As soon as I'm settled I'll wire you with my details and we can begin transferring my funds to America."

"As you wish. Might I say, Madam, that it has been a pleasure serving you these few years. If you should decide to return—"

"You'll be the first person I contact."

At the first light of morning on the day of their departure, Victoria calls for a carriage and within an hour, they are underway. Mrs. Mayfair is particularly animated at the prospect of a new home.

"This is quite an adventure. America may be a nice change of pace for us both, Victoria. After all, my Wilton's been gone for nearly twenty years now and we were never blessed with children. Other than Clayton, I've got no real ties here and he can look after himself."

"How long were you married to Wilton?"

"I met Wilton Mayfair when I was just sixteen. We were married a few months later. We were together twenty years before he was lost at sea. It was right after that I went to work for Mr. Bergeron."

Victoria pats Mrs. Mayfair's hand then gives her a kiss on the cheek.

"You've been more of a mother to me than my own mother ever was — even though I met you when I was fifty. You've never judged me."

"I'd have been proud to have a daughter like you. You made your mistakes, but you learned from 'em and made something of yourself anyway. That counts for a lot in my book."

They ride in silence, until they come within view of the steamer ships.

"We're really leaving, aren't we?"

Victoria puts her arm around Mrs. Mayfair's shoulder and gives her a squeeze. "Yes, we are."

They arrange for their luggage to be taken aboard then

Victoria stands for a few minutes looking back toward London. Mrs. Mayfair joins her.

"Not easy, is it?"

"There's not a lot I'm going to miss, to be honest. It's just that it's finally sinking in that I'm going to put all this behind me and start over brand new. It's a little overwhelming."

"I'll be there for you, dear. We can look out for one another from now on."

Victoria kisses her on the cheek. "Agreed."

Bergeron enters Stepney & Sons and removes his hat.

"I need to speak to Mr. Stepney. Tell him Mr. Bergeron is calling."

"Mr. Stepney has been dead these ten years. I'm Jeffery, may I help you?"

"Are you one of his sons?"

"Mr. Stepney didn't have any sons, sir. Just the one daughter."

"Then why is this establishment called Stepney & Sons?"

Jeffery pauses and thinks it over. "I believe Mr. Stepney was one of the sons and retained the name after he took over the shop from his father."

Bergeron takes a moment to ponder this. "A few days ago, a woman representing herself as Allison Stepney appeared at my house looking for Victoria Seely who no longer resides there. I want to know what business she had with Miss Seely. Is she available?"

"I'm afraid not, sir. Miss Stepney has left the country on an extended holiday, and she gave no indication as to when she'll return. Seeing as how she made me a partner in this establishment several days ago, and transferred the managerial responsibilities to me, I assume she's going to be gone for a while, though."

Bergeron emits a low growl. "Then you are telling me that in addition to there being no sons, there's also no one named Stepney currently involved in the running of this establishment which bears their name."

"That would be an accurate assessment sir. Would you like to leave your card?"

"No, I would not. I plan to return home and forget about this idiotic adventure as quickly as possible." He heads toward the door and places his hat back on his head. "Good day."

"Good day, sir."

Bergeron exits but re-enters a few minutes later and returns to the counter.

"Yes sir?"

"How much are the handkerchiefs?"

"Two pence for a lot of four, sir."

"Are they silk?"

"They are sir."

"Then give me four lots."

Victoria and Mrs. Mayfair stand on the deck of their steamer ship as it passes through the Narrows, and watch as the Statue of Liberty comes into view. They disembark at Ellis Island and head into the processing center. There's a long line of arrivals, so it takes them nearly an hour to get to an agent who has a book in front of him.

Mrs. Mayfair supplies the requested information. "Elizabeth Mayfair. Age forty-six, departed from London, England."

Victoria stops at the agent who asks for her name.

She glances at Mrs. Mayfair with a smile. "Victoria Wells."

Mrs. Mayfair looks at her in surprise as Victoria gives her age as twenty-two and provides her point of departure.

As soon as they leave the agent's desk, Mrs. Mayfair pauses. "Victoria Wells?"

"Has a nice ring to it don't you think, Elizabeth?"

Mrs. Mayfair's eyes tear up a bit. "It surely does, Victoria. It surely does."

West Side

THE PHOTOBOOK OF RUTH

Ruth Marshall loves mornings in New York; that stretch of time between when the first rays of the sun start peeking over the horizon up to the point when the city starts to awaken. The air has a freshness that's not evident at any other point in the day and Ruth enjoys taking long walks along the avenues where she's practically the only one around. She never feels unsafe or threatened regardless of where she ventures.

Ruth is twenty and in her third year of studies at Barnard College and generally fearless when it comes to navigating her new home. She's tall and robust with a quick gait that intimidates some people, but she's equally cheerful, with a disarming sense of humor and a quick wit. She's wearing a dark, knee-length cotton skirt with a sleeveless white button-up blouse and a well-worn Dodger's ball cap turned backwards with dark blond locks peeking out in back. This morning, she's also armed with her camera, hoping to catch some shots from around the financial district and the shoreline.

Arriving at Battery Park, Ruth snaps a few shots of boats and the statue of Liberty with the early morning sunlight hitting it then turns to head back uptown. Not far from her, seated on a wall holding a bottle of what looks like champagne, is a tiny, red-haired woman dressed in dark slacks and a red silk blouse with a medium-length light-colored duster overtop and a scarf around her neck. The woman is dressed much better than many of the homeless people Ruth has encountered. After some consideration, she cautiously approaches the woman.

"Are you okay?" The woman looks at Ruth, throwing her arms out to the side. "Because I saw you sitting here, and you don't look very happy."

"I have nothing but happiness in my life right now. I'll have you know I'm celebrating."

"What are you celebrating?"

"I'm celebrating the day. I'm celebrating my best friend who's not with me anymore." She staggers to her feet. "And I'm celebrating because it's my birthday!" She hoists the bottle into the air then finishes off what's left in it.

"Happy birthday. Do you mind if I ask how old you are?"

The woman sits on the wall again, drops her hands onto her legs, allowing the bottle to drop to the pavement. "If my poor excuse for a mother was telling me the truth and wasn't saying coronation when she meant ascension then today, I am one hundred years old. Otherwise, I'm a hundred and one and it's not my birthday."

Ruth shakes her head. "Well, you look very good for your age."

"Don't I though?" The woman looks up at Ruth and extends her hand. "I'm Victoria."

"Ruth." She shakes Victoria's hand.

"You have a few minutes to spend with a really good-looking centenarian?" She pats the wall beside her.

"Sure." Ruth leans against the wall next to her, wary but also captivated by this strange little woman. "What happened to your friend?"

Victoria looks at the ground as she ruminates over this. "She lived a full life, that's what happened. Eighty-two years and as far as I know, she never had an unkind word for anyone. She was like my mother. No, strike that. She was better than my mother because she stuck around. Of course, I say she was like a mother to me, even though I was older."

"Oh, right, you're one hundred, or maybe a hundred and one."

"You say that like I'm crazy. My mother — the real one, the bad one — told me I was born on Coronation day, when Victoria ascended to the throne. But did she mean her ascension in 1837 or her coronation in 1838? Who knows? Just one more little detail Mom left out."

"I take it you can't ask her?"

Victoria looks down, her hair falling all around her face and shakes her head. "No, that won't work. My mother drank herself to death about two days after she dumped me and my sister Amanda off at the orphanage. And that was just a few days after she most likely dumped my sister Sarah in the Thames. Left poor Billy to fend for himself. Billy's my brother. Half-brother, I guess, since dear old Mom was somewhat casual with her acquaintances after Billy's father died."

"Where's Billy now?"

Victoria looks at her with a scrunched-up face. "Haven't you been paying attention? Billy's not around anymore. He was older than I am and unfortunately didn't get whatever it is I got. He died in Bishopsgate in 1899." She smiles. "But at least I got to be with him toward the end. I lost so many years with him while he was married."

"Why is that?"

"His wife didn't want a filthy whore hanging around her family." Victoria stares ahead, and winces as though she's hearing the words as she says them.

"Why would she say something like that?"

"Because at the time she said it that's what I was. I guess I've come a long way since then. Longer than I could have imagined."

Ruth looks at her with concern and touches her shoulder. "Look, I don't know you and I really don't understand what you're talking about, but is there something I can do for you?"

Victoria bobs her head emphatically. "You can—" She rises and begins singing loudly and off-key. "Show me the way to go home, I'm tired and I want to go to bed."

Ruth stands and takes Victoria's arm as she continues singing and leads her toward the subway.

"You'll need to tell me where you live."

"Take the A-train. Uptown."

Under her breath Ruth says, "Hope you don't start singing that."

Victoria continues singing as they descend into the subway station. "Show me the way to go home."

She's still singing as they disembark at Columbus Circle. "Indicate the way to my abode, I'm fatigued, and I want to retire."

"Where's your place?"

Victoria stops, and points North on Central Park West.

"You're not going to sing anymore are you?"

"What? You don't like my singing?"

"I just think a hundred and fifty choruses are enough."

As they approach Victoria's building, Ruth is impressed. "This is a nice place. Who owns it?"

"I own the building and my place on the top floor. The units themselves are owned by the residents."

At the front door, they are met by a young Chinese man. He nods to Victoria. "Morning Miss Wells."

"Morning Peter. I heard you got into City College."

"I did. Thanks for the recommendation."

Inside an Arab man, who looks to be in his fifties, is reading a paper. He also greets Victoria.

"How's the job hunt going, Assad?"

"Very well ma'am. I have many prospects."

Victoria nods. "Remember, if there's anything I can do—"

Assad gives her the okay sign.

At the elevator, they are met by a Black man with a young girl who greets Victoria with a big smile.

"Morning Miss Wells."

Victoria gives her a hug.

"Morning Cassie. Is your Dad taking you to the zoo today?"

"Yes ma'am."

Her father places his hand on her shoulder. "We're going to get some breakfast first, though."

"Well, you have fun, okay?"

"I was so sorry to hear about Mrs. Mayfair."

Victoria pats his shoulder. "Thanks Harold. She didn't suffer."

On the elevator, Ruth seems surprised. "All those people live here?"

"Yes. I lived in this building many years ago and it was restricted. Worst bunch of people I've ever had to deal with." Victoria considers this. "Okay, maybe not the worst, but bad, nonetheless. In 1922 I bought it and made it unrestricted."

"That was a rather bold move. How'd the city take that?"

"About how you'd expect them to. But I threatened to sue on the grounds that restricted housing was unconstitutional and told them I was prepared to take it to the Supreme Court if necessary. Faced with the prospect of having to open all their buildings, they decided to concede this one. The neighbors in other buildings don't like it, but they're willing to live with it for the same reason. The residents are all hard-working, law-abiding citizens, so really, what's there to complain about?"

They exit on the top floor and Victoria hands Ruth the key.

"I'm still a little shaky."

Inside, Ruth is overwhelmed by the size of the place. "This sure beats student housing."

"Where are you studying?" Victoria walks to a credenza that's filled with pictures.

"Barnard. I'm studying Chemistry."

"That's an odd major for a woman. Most women your age are studying homemaking and husband-hunting."

"That's not really a priority for me."

Victoria grabs a framed picture from the credenza and takes it to the couch, where she sits and props her feet on the coffee table.

"There she is." Victoria holds the photo out toward Ruth. "Elizabeth Mayfair, my best friend ever."

Ruth walks over and takes the photo from her. It's a picture of Victoria and an older woman that appears to be from the turn of the century.

Ruth notes the clothing. "When was this picture taken?"

"That was when we came to America in aught two." Victoria points at a framed picture on a shelf behind Ruth. "That one was taken last year."

Ruth retrieves the other photo and is stunned to find Victoria with the same woman as in the first photo only much older.

"Wait. How can you look the same in two pictures taken thirty-six years apart?"

"I told you, I'm a hundred years old." Before Ruth can question her further, Victoria passes out.

Ruth returns the photos to their respective locations and takes the opportunity to look around. She's impressed by the number and diversity of paintings she sees then stops to look at a photo of an incredibly beautiful dancer, framed and hanging away from the others. In the back of the row of pictures on the credenza is a large sepia-toned photo of Victoria. Ruth picks it up and looks over it. The clothing appears to be from the previous century.

Ruth removes the backing of the frame it's in and finds the words "Studios Gautier de Photographie, Paris" are stamped on back. Below this, in pencil, is the date 28 June 1893. She replaces the back of the frame and closely examines the picture. What stands out is the scar on Victoria's neck which is clearly visible despite the necklace she's wearing. Ruth looks at it then over to Victoria, who appears to be sound asleep. She sets the photo down and creeps over to Victoria then bends down and lightly tugs at the collar of her shirt.

"If you want to see it, just ask." Victoria speaks blankly without opening her eyes. This startles Ruth.

"Oh, I was just—"

Without opening her eyes, Victoria unbuttons her blouse and opens it then removes her scarf, exposing the scar on her neck.

"Happy?"

"How did you—"

Victoria opens her eyes and sits up and speaks with a thick Cockney accent. "It was the Ripper! I met the Ripper and lived to tell about it. Dark Annie Chapman weren't so lucky."

She falls back onto the couch and closes her eyes again.

Ruth points toward the door. "I think I should go."

"If you must."

Ruth opens the door, but before she can leave, Victoria calls to her. "Ruth?"

She looks to see Victoria sitting up.

"Thanks for everything. I owe you one."

"No problem."

THE PHOTOBOOK OF RUTH

Victoria and Ruth approach the entrance of the extended care facility in Bay Ridge, Brooklyn but pause outside the main doors. Ruth is now sixty and while she still has a youthful face, her hair has gone mostly white with some grey flecks and her shoulders have a bit of a slump to them. She's wearing a blue dress with a light jacket over top of it and thick glasses with wire frames. Victoria is dressed in jeans and a knit turtleneck with a white denim jacket.

"You're sure you want to go through with this?" Victoria says. "We could hire another nurse."

"I don't want another nurse." Ruth is very agitated. "The last one was out smoking while I nearly burned down your apartment. When she was around she was always trying to talk to me. Asking me how I was all the time and getting in my way."

"That's why she was there."

"She wasn't always there." Tears come to her eyes. "I hate being a burden to you. You shouldn't have to spend all your free time looking after me."

"I don't mind, Dearest. I like looking after you."

"Like when I got lost downtown last week? Or when I forgot which train I needed to take, or when I had that panic attack in Macy's? I bet that was a barrel of laughs."

"I can handle it, Dearest." Victoria rubs Ruth's shoulders.

Ruth shakes her head. "You shouldn't have to. That's why we're here."

Victoria nods, then composes herself as does Ruth. "We're clear on what our story is, correct?"

"Yes. But you do the talking. I'm less likely to get confused if I don't have to say anything."

Victoria nods then takes Ruth's arm, and they enter and check in at the main desk. They are met by Mr. Feinstein, the associate director.

"Ms. Marshall and Ms. Wells. Good to see you again. We have some paperwork to take care of then we can get Ms. Marshall settled."

"Sounds good. Mom, does that sound good to you?"

"Yes." Ruth looks around, and suddenly seems as

149

though she is not certain where she is.

Feinstein shows them to his office, where Victoria outlines the financial arrangements. "This account will be funded specifically for Mom's care. The bank will draft a check to you once a month. If there's ever any interruption, however, and you're unable to reach me, I've given my accountant, Mr. Ferguson at Montgomery Trust, conditional power of attorney to act on my behalf and he'll see that the amount is taken care of promptly."

"Very good, Ms. Wells."

"Now I'll be here as much as I can throughout the week, and can handle any concerns at that time. However, if there are any emergencies, please don't hesitate to call me day or night. Here are my numbers."

"We'll keep this information in her file. We also ask that you include any final arrangements. In case we're unable to reach you in a timely manner."

Victoria closes her eyes and takes a deep breath.

"Yes. I have that information here."

Feinstein looks over the paperwork. "It seems everything is in order. Now let's see about getting your mother settled in, shall we?"

As they walk through the hall, Mr. Feinstein gives them an overview of the arrangements. "As you may remember from the tour, the rooms are very warm and comfortable. This is designed to give our residents the feel of being at home or in a nice hotel rather than a care facility. In fact, most of our residents need only the least amount of constant care, though we do keep them closely monitored for their safety."

"Did you receive the bedding we sent over for Mom?" Victoria says, smiling at Ruth.

"We did and the staff has gotten the room set up just as you requested. She should detect only a few minor differences from the room she's used to being in and in a few days, those differences shouldn't be noticed."

They arrive at Ruth's room and enter. Victoria is uplifted as she looks around at the accommodations. It's almost identical to the room Ruth was using at Victoria's apartment, though a bit smaller. She looks at Ruth who also appears pleased.

Mr. Feinstein steps to the door. "Well, I'll give you two time to get Ms. Marshall settled in and if you need anything, just press one of the buttons on the wall or by the bed."

Once he's gone, Victoria hugs Ruth. "I have a much better feeling about this now. It's gorgeous."

"See, I told you things would be okay."

Several days after meeting Victoria, Ruth stops in to see a former professor who lived in Paris for a while after the war and who shares Ruth's interest in photography.

"Did you ever hear of a picture studio called Gautier?"

"Gautier? Yes, I've heard of it. I tried to get a job there. It was a very well-known studio. Why are you asking?"

"I met someone the other night and she told me a very weird story. She was kind of out of it, so I helped her get home. She had a picture of herself and on back it said it was taken at Gautier Studios in 1893."

"Certainly possible. They were in business from around 1885 through 1922, I believe. How old was this person?"

"That's the weird part. She looks like she's in her early twenties, but when I met her, she said she was a hundred years old."

"That is weird. But, if the Gautier photo is genuine, she couldn't be much younger than early-sixties, assuming she was in her late teens to early twenties when she posed for it."

"I know. Science major. I did the math. That's crazy isn't it?"

"It's definitely within the realm of possibility, but not probability. Maybe it's a relative, like her mother or grandmother."

"I thought the same thing. But—" She hesitates.

"But what?"

"She has a scar."

"A scar?"

"The woman in the picture has a scar on her neck, like

someone cut her throat at some time. The woman I met has a similar scar on her neck."

The professor leans forward. "Are you suggesting that there's a young woman running around New York who sat for a photo in 1893 and hasn't changed since? Sounds like someone's trying to hoodwink you, Ruth."

"Maybe, but she also had a photo that was taken with a friend of hers in 1902 and another one with the same friend taken a year or so ago. The friend obviously looks older, but she doesn't." Ruth throws her hands up to stop him from responding. "Let's say she's telling the truth, or believes she is. How could I prove or disprove it?"

"Has she given you any facts? If so, you could compare what she says with what the record says. It wouldn't prove it beyond a shadow of a doubt, but it would lend some weight to her story."

Ruth thinks about it. "Yes, she's given me some facts. She says she came here in 1902 with her friend. She also told me her brother died in England in 1899, but I only have his first name."

The professor waves a hand in Ruth's direction. "There you go. Immigration records are on file at the federal building. If you can't access them directly, you should at least be able to find an index that might tell you what you need to know. As for the brother, parish records in England are held by the Records Office, so maybe they could verify that portion."

Ruth taps the desk. "Thanks a lot. You've given me some good ideas."

She leaves and heads across campus to her lab. Outside the science building, she's surprised to find Victoria leaning against a wall.

"Victoria? How'd you find me?"

"I just asked where I could find women studying Chemistry and they pointed me in this direction."

"Why have you tracked me down?"

"I thought I'd ask you out to lunch. Maybe give you an opportunity to get to know me when I'm not wallowing in self-pity."

"You're not going to sing are you?"

"Maybe just a hundred choruses this time."

Ruth pitches her head toward the entrance. "Come on. I'll show you where I do my husband hunting."

After a tour of the lab, Ruth takes Victoria by the dorms, and they stop at her room. A shapely woman with dark hair and a tanned complexion emerges from a back room and greets Ruth, in a slightly seductive tone. "Hey you." Seeing Victoria, she changes her tone. "Oh. Ruth. You have company."

Ruth motions between them. "Victoria Wells, this is Cindy Morelli, my roommate." She emphasizes the word "roommate".

Victoria addresses Cindy. "Nice to meet you. I've asked Ruth to join me for lunch. Would you like to come along?"

Cindy looks at Ruth, then back to Victoria. "Sure, I guess."

At the cafe, Victoria chats with Ruth about various topics while Cindy nervously listens in, contributing when asked a question, but otherwise saying very little. When the food comes, she picks at it, while constantly shooting glances at Ruth.

Victoria leans toward them and speaks just above a whisper. "If I'm being presumptuous, just tell me, but you two aren't just roommates, are you?"

Ruth glances at Cindy, who gives her a shocked expression, then looks away. "No, we're not."

"Ruth!" Cindy speaks in a forceful whisper.

Victoria lays her hand on the table. "It's okay. Good for you both. I totally understand keeping it quiet."

Cindy relaxes a bit.

Ruth seizes the opportunity to change the subject. "That brother you told me about the other night, what's his name?"

Victoria narrows one eye. "Why would you want to know that?"

"Just curious."

Victoria gives her a sly grin. "Curious. Sure. His name was William Seely, that's S-E-E-L-Y, though how it may have been recorded is anyone's guess. He married his wife Bess in 1869. Never knew her full name and never much cared. He had two sons, Donald, and Willem. I'm pretty sure they're gone by now, but you never know. They wouldn't be much help anyway. I only met Donald once and gave him a fake name then. Oh, and my name was Seely when I left England too. I changed it at Ellis Island." She stops, and gives Ruth a curious stare. "Are you going to write this down?"

"Don't need to." Ruth taps her head. "My mind's like a steel trap."

"Impressive. I'd recommend you check out whatever police records are there as well, but you probably wouldn't like what you find in them. Plus I'd only be listed as Vickie or a person of interest if at all."

Cindy looks from one to the other. "What are you two talking about?"

"Just a little research project. Right Ruth?"

"Right you are. Should be fun."

Victoria is walking toward her building one afternoon when she spots Ruth walking aimlessly along, her hands in her jacket pockets, apparently troubled by something.

"Ruth?"

"Victoria, I didn't think I'd run into you."

"You're practically in front of my building."

"I guess I just wasn't paying attention."

"Is something wrong?"

"Cindy left school. Moved back with her parents and won't return my calls. Her mom told me Cindy's engaged and asked me to stop calling."

"That's terrible."

"I talked to her brother a short while ago, and he told me that their parents heard some rumors about me and Cindy and demanded she move back with them. After that her old boyfriend showed up and they started going out again."

"You're still on good terms with her brother?"

"I've always been on pretty good terms with Gino. He told me he didn't exactly understand what was going on between me and her, but he thought I was okay and felt I deserved the full story. He even suggested we catch a Dodgers game together sometime."

Victoria takes Ruth's arm. "Come on up, we can talk about it."

"Are you sure?"

"I owe you one, remember? I'm nothing if not a sympathetic ear."

Inside, Victoria pours a glass of wine for her and Ruth. Victoria sits on a bench along the wall facing the paintings as Ruth examines the artwork.

"I am very impressed with your collection." She points to the Picasso. "How did you come by this one?"

Victoria rises and goes over. She stands sideways, looking at the painting over her left shoulder. "Pablo painted it for me in Paris around 1918."

"Pablo Picasso?"

"No, Pablo Parker. Of course Picasso. He needed money and I told him that I'd give him some in exchange for a painting. The next day, he brought me this." She leans closer to the painting. "He signed it for me." She points to the lower right corner.

Ruth looks to see the words "Para Victoria" written above his signature.

Victoria walks over to the piano. "He told me it's supposed to capture my inner essence, but I don't see it."

Victoria sits at the piano and begins running scales up and down.

"I need to get the tuner in here this week."

She starts playing a section of Rhapsody in Blue.

"You know Gershwin?"

"Knew him." She stops. "Oh, wait, you meant the music, right?"

"You knew George Gershwin?"

"I did. When he finally got around to writing down the piano score for Rhapsody, he asked several pianists to come over and try it out. I was there, Oscar Levant, some others." She shakes her head. "Terrible loss, just like when Scott died."

"Scott?"

155

"Joplin." Victoria breaks into the Maple Leaf Rag. "I met him once. There's a photo of me with him somewhere around here."

"How long have you been playing?" Ruth leans against the piano.

"Since 1888. I picked it up fairly quickly."

Ruth takes a sip of her wine and moves a bit closer to Victoria. "Speaking of which, I did a little research on you."

"Did you?" Victoria keeps playing.

"Something you said the other night stuck in my head. You said, 'Dark Annie Chapman wasn't so lucky. I looked up a listing of Jack the Ripper's victims and it said that Annie Chapman was sometimes called Dark Annie. I suppose you could have looked that up, but the way you said it sounded like you were used to calling her that."

Victoria laughs. "I knew Dark Annie. She could be very pleasant when she wasn't plastered out of her mind, which was a lot. Then you just steered clear. I knew Cathy Eddowes, Long Liz Stride, and I sort of knew Mary Jane Kelly. The Ripper butchered her. It scared the hell out of all the girls at the time, but fear doesn't pay the rent."

"I talked to a professor of mine who lived in Paris after the war, and he remembers Gautier photographic studios. I also went down to the Federal building and checked the indices for immigrants in 1902 and there you were."

Victoria nods.

Ruth holds up her hand. "Understand, I'm not willing to commit to one hundred just yet." She paces away from the piano. "I had a great aunt who made it to a hundred and one and she didn't look anything like you. But you're older than you appear."

Victoria stops playing and places her hands onto the bench. "Once you've committed yourself to the idea why is one hundred so difficult? If I was going to lie about it, the slow aging part would be the real whopper. I could just as easily have said seventy-five or one twenty-seven."

"I guess you're right. Still, it's a lot to get your head around. I'm a scientist. I need facts. Like that scar. Did you really get it from Jack the Ripper?"

Victoria starts playing Rhapsody in Blue again. "I never said I was attacked by the Ripper, just by someone pretending to be the Ripper."

"You're sure the man who attacked you wasn't the Ripper."

"I lived in his house for fourteen years afterward. I'm sure it would have come up at some point."

"That doesn't make any sense. Why would you move in with someone who did that to you?"

"I was very different back then. I believed I could make a deal with the devil and not get burned." Her voice cracks. "But you always get burned."

She rises and shoves the bench under the piano then goes to the couch and sits down, folding her legs under her.

"Enough about me. We're here to talk about you."

Ruth joins her on the couch. "Yeah, me and my love life." She sets her wine on the table in front of her and leans back. "I guess I'm not surprised how the situation with Cindy turned out. She was very eager when we were behind closed doors, but out in public, she was always very nervous and self-conscious." While she's talking, Victoria moves a bit closer to her and props an arm on the back of the couch. "We ran into a friend of hers from Brooklyn once when we were out window shopping and I thought Cindy was going to jump out of her skin. We weren't holding hands or showing any affection, just walking along laughing about the new styles."

"Was she always like that?"

"She was whenever we went out." She shakes her head. "I guess I always knew it wasn't going to work out. Maybe I just thought I'd be wrong." She pats Victoria's hand. "It's really nice to have someone I can talk to about these things."

"You can always talk to me." She leans over and hugs Ruth. She starts to sit back but stops and leans in and kisses Ruth who starts out a bit unsure then warms to the kiss. Victoria pulls away. "If I'm wrong, tell me."

"As soon as you're wrong, I will."

They kiss again.

A few hours later they are lying in bed, Ruth on her back with her head resting on one arm and Victoria on her side with her head propped on her hand.

"So much for husband hunting," Ruth says.

Gino Morelli sits on the stoop of his family's row house in Brooklyn, waiting for his friend Jimmy to show up so they can go to the game. Gino has invited a couple of others along and he's not sure how Jimmy will react to them. As he sits there, Tony Greco, his older sister's fiancé, arrives with some flowers and says hello as he goes up the steps. A moment or so later, Mrs. Morelli greets Tony with compliments and platitudes and admits him to the apartment.

From down the road, he hears a familiar whistle, and he looks to see his pal Jimmy Falcone strolling along with his hands in his pockets. Gino gets up and calls toward the open window.

"Ma, Jimmy's here. We're leaving."

Jimmy stops in front of Gino's rowhouse.

"Hey wise guy, what took you so long?" Gino playfully whacks Jimmy on the back of the head. "I told you to get here before Tony did."

"I'm here now. What's the big deal?"

"I don't want him or Cindy grilling us about what we're doing today."

"We're going to the game. Again I say, what's the big deal?" He considers it a minute. "Oh, wait. You didn't tell them we was meeting those girls, right?"

"No and I don't want you saying nothing either. It's not like we're going out with them."

"So, what are we doing?"

"We're going and they're going and we're sitting together and that's about it."

"Sounds to me like we're going with a lot of women in that case. Are we even sitting in the same row?"

"Of course we're sitting in the same row."

He and Jimmy take the subway headed toward Flat-bush.

"So we're meeting some girls who we aren't on a date with, and you don't want your family to know anything about it." He mulls it over for a moment. "Say, is this that girl your sister was messing around with at school?" Gino doesn't immediately respond. "Aw, Gino, what are you doing? Your parents would go nuts if they found out about this."

"I know. Which is why we ain't telling them about it." Jimmy shakes his head. "Look, I don't know what Ruth and Cindy were doing. I don't care. Ruth's a great girl, a lot of fun. She loves the Dodgers and knows a heck of a lot about baseball history and stats. I'm not going there to marry her. I'm going to watch a game with her."

"Okay. So who's this other girl?"

"Her name's Victoria. I think she's Ruth's, ah, friend."

"Friend like Cindy was her friend?"

"Yeah, something like that."

Jimmy throws his arm around Gino's neck and pulls his head down then grinds his knuckles into it.

"You're lucky you're my best friend. Otherwise, I'd knock your block off."

Laughing, Gino fights him off. "Cut it out, will you?"

At Ebbets Field, Gino spots Ruth near one of the entrances and waves. Beside her is a small woman whose hair appears to be a light red color. She's wearing women's style casual slacks and a light jacket and has a silk scarf around her neck.

As he and Jimmy approach, Ruth says, "Hey, Gino. Good to see you."

Gino nods then points his thumb at Jimmy. "This is my pal, Jimmy Falcone."

"Pleasure."

Ruth indicates her companion. "This is Victoria, and she's attending her first baseball game."

"Hey, you're in for a treat." Gino points between Ruth and Jimmy. "Between these two, you have a walking encyclopedia of baseball."

Inside the stadium, Ruth and Victoria sit between Gino and Jimmy so that Ruth's to Jimmy's left and Victoria is to Gino's right. Ruth and Jimmy immediately launch into a highly detailed discussion about the Dodger's recent acquisitions which Victoria finds hard to follow. Gino spots a hotdog vendor and taps Victoria's shoulder. "Say, you want a dog, Victoria?"

"The kind you eat, right?"

"Of course." Gino chuckles and signals to the vendor. Victoria indicates she'll take one. Gino pays for them. "So, Victoria, you go to school with Ruth?"

"No, I pretty much went to the school of hard knocks, with some private tutoring for a few years."

"Must be nice. I'm getting out in a couple of months, and I won't miss it a bit."

"College not in your future?"

He shrugs. "I suppose I could go. My folks saved a bunch when Cindy dropped out, but I like working with my hands, fixing things. I'm not much of a thinker."

"There's always vocational school."

He points at her. "Yeah, that's what I'm looking into. The way this city's growing, a welder or a metal worker could make a good living."

"I suppose that's true. A lot of people are worried there'll be another war in Europe."

"If it happens, it happens. I don't have any say one way or the other."

"Kind of a roll with the punches kind of guy, eh."

"You know it."

The game starts and their conversation breaks off. Occasionally when something happens on the field, Ruth leans toward Victoria and explains what happened. In the fifth inning, Dolph Camilli is up to bat. On the third pitch, the sharp crack of the bat is heard along with the roar of the crowd. The ball heads in their direction, then, when it's just over their heads and dropping, Jimmy springs up and catches it bare-handed. He holds it above his head and pumps his other fist. Gino pats him on the back as does Ruth.

Victoria leans toward Ruth. "I take it that's a good thing, right?"

"Very good."

Still standing, Jimmy points at Gino. "I'm going to get

Camilli to sign it."

After the game Victoria realizes she's left her jacket in the stands and goes to retrieve it. Gino, Ruth, and Jimmy wait near the players' entrance until Dolph Camilli exits.

"Hey Dolph, I caught your homer. Could I get you to sign it for me?"

"Sure, kid." Ruth hands him a pen. Camilli signs it and hands it back. "Here you go."

"Thanks!" Jimmy, Ruth, and Gino start walking, and Jimmy tosses the ball in the air a couple of times. On one toss, he misses it, and it rolls away toward a large man in a brown coat. The man picks it up and looks at it.

"Hey buddy could you toss me that ball?"

The man looks at him, laughs and puts the ball in his pocket. Jimmy runs over. "Hey, that's my ball! I caught it."

"Finders' keepers squirt. Now beat it." He starts to walk away. Jimmy starts after him, but Gino blocks him.

"Jimmy, that guy's built like a brick wall. He'll murder you."

"What's going on?" Victoria says as she walks up.

"Jimmy dropped the game ball he just got signed by the best slugger on the team and that big palooka over there snatched it up and won't give it back," Ruth says.

"You mean the guy in the brown coat." Victoria eyes him closely.

"Yeah, that's the guy," Jimmy says.

Victoria thinks about it for a second. "Did you see which pocket he put it in?"

Ruth says, "Left coat pocket."

Victoria nods. "Why don't you guys head on to the train. I'll meet you there in a few minutes."

"What are you going to do?" Gino says.

"I just need to pick something up."

Ruth, Gino, and a very distraught Jimmy head for the train. Victoria walks quickly after the guy in the brown coat.

Several minutes later, the trio are milling around the entrance to the train when Victoria walks up. "Ready?"

"Where'd you go?" Gino says.

"Just wanted to make sure I wasn't leaving anything else behind."

They board the train. Jimmy continues to berate himself for losing the ball.

"I am so stupid. If I'd just kept the darn thing in my pocket I'd still have it."

"You're talking about the ball, right?" Victoria says.

"Yes, I'm talking about the ball."

"I didn't get a good look at it, what does one of those things look like up close?"

"Are you serious?" Gino says. "They're white, stitched up, baseball logo on it. This one had a signature on one side."

Victoria pulls a baseball from her coat pocket. "Sort of like this?"

Jimmy's eyes widen. "No, it's not. Is it?"

"See for yourself." Victoria hands him the ball. He takes it and looks it over. The blemish from where the bat hit it is there and on the other side is Dolph Camilli's signature."

"How the heck did you do that?" Jimmy puts the ball in his coat pocket. "I'm taking no chances this time. How did you do that?"

She leans forward and gives him a quick hug. "Don't worry about it."

Ruth looks between them, and something occurs to her. "Hey, Jimmy, let me take a look at that ball again."

Jimmy reaches into his pocket, but the ball isn't there.

"What the—"

"Looking for this?" Victoria holds up the ball.

"I'll be." Jimmy points his finger at her. "I better keep my eye on you."

"Say, anybody want to get sodas?" Gino says. "Anywhere but Bay Ridge."

They head over to downtown Brooklyn to a soda shop Ruth knows and take a booth inside near the rear.

"You sure you never went here with Cindy?" Gino says.

Ruth laughs. "No, she always wanted to go to this place near campus. I stop in here whenever I walk over the bridge."

Jimmy looks back and forth between Victoria and Ruth. "So do you two live together?"

Gino throws up his hands. "Why you asking them about that?"

"No, that's okay. Ruth lives in student housing, and I live in a building I own on Central Park West."

"That's a pretty high rent area isn't it?" Gino says.

"Not when you own the place."

"So how does a person your age afford a building on the upper west side?" Jimmy says.

"I'm older than I look for one thing. But I also work in the music business, both as a performer and manager and I own my own record label, Mon Amour."

Jimmy nods. "I've heard of them, Jazz, right?"

"Mainly."

"Yeah, a lot of groups nobody's heard of, but they sound pretty good," Jimmy says.

"That's about it. They sign with us then, when they get popular, they jump ship and go for the big bucks. The industry's changing a lot anyway, so business has been thinning out a bit."

"So, what are you going to do?" Gino says.

"Probably fold up the label for now then revive it down the road if things swing back in our direction. We've always been a small label that caters to a pretty specific clientele."

They continue to talk as they finish their sodas. Finally, Jimmy and Gino walk Ruth and Victoria to the subway.

"Thanks to you both for being perfect gentlemen," Ruth says.

"Yeah, it was good talking to you," Jimmy says to Ruth. "You want to talk baseball anytime, look me up."

"I will," Ruth says.

"Yeah, let's do it again sometime," Gino says.

"Sure thing," Victoria says. "I could use another lesson."

Victoria has business which takes her to Los Angeles for more than a week. Upon her return, she checks in with Ruth in the extended care facility. The nurse shows Victoria to Ruth's room.

"Ruth, look who's here. It's your daughter."

"I don't have a daughter." Ruth seems, very agitated. "I told you I don't have a daughter. Stop telling me I do."

Victoria goes to her and takes her hands.

"It's Victoria. Don't you remember me?"

Ruth stares at her for several minutes, then a look of recognition crosses her face, and she touches Victoria's face. "Vickie?"

"That's me."

"Where are we? What is this place? I want to go home."

"I know you do. But you need someone who can look after you."

"I'm scared."

Victoria wraps her arms around Ruth. "It's okay."

"Why do they say you're my daughter? Why do they keep telling me I have a daughter. I don't have any children."

"We're pretending, remember?" Victoria looks at the nurse and winks. "We're pretending I'm your daughter today."

Ruth shakes her head. "I don't remember anything. Can't you get me out of here?"

"Not now. Maybe soon, though."

Victoria sits with her until Ruth drops off to sleep. When she steps out into the hallway to look for a nurse, Ms. Streeter, the director, is waiting.

"Could I have a word with you in my office, Ms. Wells?"

"Certainly." Victoria questions her about Ruth as they walk. "How long has Mom been like this? She seemed fine before I left."

"The nurses say it comes and goes, but she's getting to the point where it's more often during the day."

At the office, Ms. Streeter shows Victoria to a seat and sits in the chair next to her.

"We aren't equipped at this facility to provide the type of constant care your mother needs."

"I was hoping it hadn't gotten to that point yet. Now that it has, what do you suggest?"

"There are a number of excellent facilities not far from here." She hands Victoria a brochure. "This facility is located near Downtown Brooklyn and consistently scores in the top ten percent for the level of care provided. There are always doctors and nurses on hand in case of emergencies and they employ the most up-to-date systems to insure no one hurts the patients."

"Or that they don't hurt themselves."

"That's right. If you'd like, I could arrange a visit, so you could see first-hand the care your Mom would receive."

Victoria fights back tears. "That would be good."

A FAMILY AFFAIR

In the late afternoon, on the top floor of the London office of A. A. Stepney Enterprises, visitors are well advised to look both ways before leaving the elevator. Otherwise, they may find themselves diving for the first available corner to avoid being plowed down by a six-year-old speed demon. Experienced visitors know how to spot the warning signs alerting them to take cover.

First, they'll hear a faint squeaking which modulates quickly from high to low then a whirring sound followed by a slight rumble. This is all followed by a child's voice saying "Beep, beep! Beep, beep!" Then around the corner comes a tiny girl with dark hair riding a tricycle as fast as her legs can propel it, which most will agree is surprisingly fast. When people are in the hallway she'll zigzag around them, cutting them off at corners as she heads off on yet another turn of the floor. Her name is Sylvia and she's the only child of current CEO Walter Bowman, whose father, Peter, is the surviving son of Jeffery Bowman, and chairman emeritus of the board.

As most business is conducted at A. A. Stepney during school hours, those most affected by Sylvia's excursions on the top floor are the employees who serve the board and executive suite. Among the more vocal of them, Sylvia's earned the nickname Damien, with others speculating on whether her head can spin a full 360° like her compatriot in The Exorcist.

More than a few swear that they're prepared to march into Walter Bowman's office and suggest he keep a tighter rein on his daughter, but their conviction wanes once it's pointed out that since his wife died two years ago, Sylvia has been Walter's entire world outside of A. A. Stepney, and he will abide no ill words about her. Those in the know will approach Allison Stepney first, which usually leads her out into the hallway with the task of nabbing Sylvia as she rushes by then finding a more suitable form of recreation for the tot until her father retrieves her for the trek home.

At the urging of a pair of secretaries who've both been nearly run down twice, Allison takes to the hallway, creeping along the wall to gain the element of surprise. When she hears Sylvia turn the far corner she peeks around the wall, just enough to be caught by Sylvia, who smiles and crouches forward in a ready position. Allison takes a few steps back, ducking behind a column then, when Sylvia rounds the corner, springs out, grabbing Sylvia under the arms and lifting her off the tricycle, which rolls to a stop a few feet away. Allison pulls Sylvia close to her face and says in a mock-chiding manner "What did your father say about riding up here?" She rubs her nose against Sylvia's then extends her arms and swings Sylvia around once, which causes the little girl to roar with laughter. Then she puts her down and sits beside her on the floor.

"Allie, can we play in your office?"

"I don't know about that. I'm very cross with you right now. People say you're running into them as you ride along."

Sylvia throws her left arm out and looks away from Allison.

"They won't get out of the way. I try to warn them, but they won't move."

"They're supposed to be here. They work here, remember? You're just visiting."

"Yes ma'am." Sylvia looks down.

Allison gives her a hug.

"You must remember to be more considerate. The people here work very hard for me and your father. Someday they may work for you, too."

"Not me. I'm going to be the Queen!"

"Queen, eh? Considering you have a continent full of nobles ahead of you, I'm not sure how you'll pull that one off."

"Allie, look." Sylvia pulls her lip upwards. "I lost another tooth."

"I see that. How'd you lose this one?"

"It just fell out. It was loose and then it just came out."

Allison nods.

Sylvia gives a frustrated sigh and sits beside Allison.

"Allie, can't we play in your office?"

"My office is a bit of a mess presently. The new fall fashions are due to go to the manufacturer in a few days and I'm only slightly ahead of schedule right now."

Sylvia drops her head onto her fist. "Papa won't be leaving for an hour or more. I don't have anything to do until then."

They sit for a few moments. "Okay, how about this. Why don't you come to my office, and you can be my assistant?"

Sylvia perks up considerably. "What would I do?"

"Whatever I need you to do, get sketch pads, sharpen pencils. You name it."

Sylvia claps. "That sounds like fun!"

Allison stands and holds out her hand for Sylvia who takes it. They pass the tricycle. "You'd better bring that or it most likely won't be here when you come back. You can park it under my drawing table."

Sylvia gets on the tricycle again and Allison pushes her along as they head to the office.

Not quite half an hour later, Peter Bowman taps on Allison's door then sticks his head in. "Miss Stepney, I hear you have a new assistant."

Looking up from her job of sorting pencils, Sylvia yells, "Grandpa!"

"Oh, yes, she's very efficient. Those markers are sorted like never before."

Peter Bowman inherited his father's hairline and general demeanor, but almost nothing else. Unlike David, who'd been a carbon copy of Jeffery, only taller, Peter sometimes reminds Allison of her father, Cedric, though Peter is nowhere near as rotund or boisterous as Cedric was. Somewhat stocky with a mild slump to his shoulders Peter gives the impression of a banker from earlier in the century rather than an executive at one of the top clothing manufacturers in the world.

Sylvia runs over to Peter, who lifts her up then gives her a kiss on the cheek. He carries her with him to a seat in front of Allison's desk and sets Sylvia on his knee once he's seated.

Glancing up at him from her sketch pad, Allison says, "Business or personal?"

Peter considers it a moment then says, "Actually, I was sort of hoping you'd determine that."

Allison looks at him with a raised eyebrow and says, "Bored are you?" Peter shrugs. "Well, I'm afraid the position of pencil sorter has been filled Mr. Bowman. What other skills do you possess?"

Peter laughs. "Well, until you're done with your part there's not much for the rest of us to do, is there?"

"You're not pinning this on me. I'm ahead of schedule for a change."

"Grandpa, look." Sylvia shows Peter her missing tooth.

Peter looks grim. "Keep that up and you won't have any before long."

He winks at Allison.

"I won't?" Sylvia sounds worried.

"Oh yes, just look at me." Peter reaches into his mouth and takes out his lower dentures. Sylvia throws her hands over her mouth with a frightened look on her face. Peter puts his dentures back in. "We'll have to fit you with a tiny pair, I suppose."

"No!" Sylvia still has her hand over her mouth.

She looks at Allison, who rolls her eyes. "Now, Peter is that any way to treat your only granddaughter? Never you worry Sylvia, they grow back."

"Do they?" Sylvia looks between Allison and Peter.

"Well, at least once," Peter says with a chuckle.

"What happened to yours?"

Allison looks up from her drawing. "He didn't take care of them, and the tooth fairy came and repossessed them."

"I'm going to take very good care of mine." Sylvia hops down from Peter's lap and crosses to the far side of the office, where photos of models wearing Allison's designs are situated.

Peter leans back and folds his hands in front of him. "Had a card from Harry."

Allison puts her arms on the desk and leans forward. "Harry. What'd he have to say?"

"General details about his retirement. He says the fishing's great in St. Augustine and he renewed his offer for me to take over the other half of his duplex."

"Did he?"

"Yes and I'm seriously considering it. I've been at this long enough. Time to let the next generation carry on."

"If you say so." Allison looks back to her designs.

"He did ask a rather odd question. He wanted to know if you had any living relatives."

"Why would he want to know that?"

"Said he visited New York a few weeks ago and attended a reception for business leaders and saw a young woman who was your twin."

"What was her name?"

"Harry said she left before the event was over and he didn't get a chance to speak to her. He asked around, though, and learned her name was Victoria Wells."

"Victoria?" Allison reacts with interest. "That's very interesting. When I was a teenager, the cops kept pinching me because they said I looked like someone named Vickie who was a pickpocket. Never got a look at her, though, as she obviously ran in different circles than I did."

She recalls her dealings with Lainie Robinson. "There was also a music teacher named Victoria. I was told by a mutual acquaintance that she and I looked a lot alike. I never met her, though we just missed one another a time or two."

She shakes her head. "This was just before I left England with Brigitte, so I'm sure she's well into her hundreds, if not long dead."

"Were you aware of any family, other than Cedric and Anne?"

"Not that I knew. I pity them if our parents were as caring of them as they were of me. If so, I doubt they made it very far."

Peter chuckles. "Wouldn't it be something if there was another one like you out there?"

Allison shakes her head. "Brigitte's the only one I've ever met, though she says she's met others. Mind you, I've come to think of her as a sister, but to have a relative like me. That's a tall order."

"Do you plan to look into this?"

"Look into what?" She turns back to her drawings. "Harry Stein, whose eyesight isn't what it used to be, caught site of some woman in the tiny hamlet of New York City who may or may not resemble me. Call the detectives."

The intercom buzzes and Walter Bowman's voice comes on. "Allison, would you know where Sylvia's gotten off to?"

Allison motions for Sylvia to come over then presses the button and nods at Sylvia. "Hello papa."

"Wonderful. Glad to hear she's in good hands. Now, do you know where my father is?"

Allison presses the talk button. "Matter of fact, I know exactly where he is."

There's a long pause. "You're not having a party in there are you?"

"Not at all. I just happen to be the designated Bowman rest stop for today."

"Well send them both this way if you don't mind. I'm ready to go home and want to have a few words with Dad before we leave."

"Right-o."

Peter rises.

"Back to the real world, I suppose," he says.

He retrieves Sylvia's tricycle from under the desk.

"What, this world not real enough for you?" Allison picks up Sylvia and gives her a hug. "Now be more careful out there." Allison shakes her finger at Sylvia. "We have enough trouble keeping employees without you mowing them down."

"Okay, Allie." She gets on her tricycle and leads her grandfather out into the hallway.

Allison sits for a moment then picks up her bag and rummages through it, finally removing a worn and yellowed slip of cardboard that's preserved in a clear plastic sleeve. On the front are the words, "Miss V. Seely, Pianist and Music Teacher", with an address.

Allison dials her assistant. "Leslie. Could you do a bit of research for me? Personal, not business. Would you see if there's a genealogical association for the Seely family – 'ee' not 'ea'."

She hangs up then turns to look out the window. "Victoria."

It is nearly four-o-clock in the morning when Gino Morelli is awakened by the phone ringing. He answers then feels around for his glasses. The voice at the other end sounds somewhat tired, and Gino can hear in the background sounds of a busy hospital.

"Gino Morelli?"

"Yeah, this is he."

"Do you know a Franco Morelli?"

"He's my son. What's this about?"

"This is Alvin Leonard at Eastern Medical Center near Patterson, New Jersey. I'm afraid there's been an accident involving your son and his family."

"What kind of accident? Are they all right?"

"Mr. Morelli, can you get here quickly?"

"What's happened to them? Why won't you tell me?"

There's a long pause. "Mr. Morelli, your grandchildren were injured in the crash. They need you now."

"Are you telling me—" Gino breaks off before he says what he already knows to be true.

"I'm afraid there were no other survivors. Mr. Morelli, can you make it here fairly soon?"

Gino sits, shaking his head, trying to keep himself together.

"Mr. Morelli?"

"Sure, I can get there. Give me the directions and I'll leave right now."

When Gino enters the emergency room of the medical center his grandchildren Theresa and Bart are sitting with two New Jersey state troopers. Seeing Gino, Theresa calls out, "Grandpa!"

She runs to him followed by Bart. He hugs them both.

"Hey, kids. You okay?"

"They won't let us see Mom and Dad," she says. There are minor cuts and bruises on both the children. "They won't tell us anything."

"What happened?" Gino says.

"We were in the back," Theresa says. "I think I was asleep because all I remember is a crash and then we were here."

"I heard one of the troopers say that somebody crossed the road going the wrong way," Bart says.

Gino walks with the kids back over to the troopers.

"Mr. Morelli?" the male trooper says. "Can I have a word with you?"

Gino nods and asks the children to stay with the female trooper.

The male trooper leads Gino away from the kids. "Your grandchildren are the only survivors from either car. But it appears that as your son and his family were driving along a state highway another car crossed into their lane and hit them. We believe the other driver was either intoxicated or fell asleep. Your son and his wife were declared dead at the scene. The children seem to have escaped injury because they were asleep in the back of the station wagon."

Gino shakes his head. "How can this happen? They were so young. They were just getting started. Can I see them?"

The trooper shakes his head.

"That's probably not a good idea just now. The entire front end of the car was demolished. The coroner will need you to make a positive ID but not right now." He flips through his notes. "We've been unable to contact your daughter-in-law's family. Would you have any information on them?"

"I only met her parents once a few years ago. I think they travel a lot. I have a contact number at home."

The trooper nods and hands him a card. "If you find out anything, let me know. I am very sorry for your loss Mr. Morelli."

Gino takes a minute to compose himself, then heads back to the children.

"Hey kids, we're going to get out of here. You can stay at my place until we get things sorted out, okay?"

"I want to see Mom and Dad," Theresa says. "Why can't we see them?"

Gino gives her a hug then asks her and Bart to sit down. Then he sits beside them and tells them what the trooper told him. They both break down and Gino puts his arms around them and holds them for a long time. Finally, they gather their things and leave with Gino.

The following week, the courts award temporary custody of the children to Gino. Six months later, after being unable to locate either of Bethany's parents, the courts name Gino the children's permanent guardian.

Victoria heads up the walkway to the assisted living facility where Ruth lives. Though she's always happy to spend time with Ruth, Victoria also dreads the visits on some level, as each time she sees a little more of Ruth slip away from her. Halfway to the door, she's met by an older, balding gentleman with an olive complexion on his way out of the facility.

He gives her a long look then stops and stares after her. "Victoria?"

She stops and turns toward him. "That's me."

He examines her up and down. "Well, I'll be."

"I'm sorry, do I know you?"

"I think so. My name's Gino Morelli. I used to know Ruth Marshall back in the thirties and forties. She sort of knew my sister first, but I'm the one who stayed in touch."

Victoria considers this a moment then gives him a smile. "Yes, Gino, I remember."

"I thought for a minute you were Victoria's daughter, but it is you, isn't it?"

"Yes it is. I guess I'm just one of the lucky ones."

"I guess you are." He shrugs. "Oh well, I've seen stranger things I suppose. Anyway, I was here visiting my aunt and saw Ruth's name on another door. So, I thought I'd stick my head in and say hello." He looks down and shakes his head. "It's real sad seeing her like that. She was always so sharp."

Victoria nods. "She has her good days and bad. Did she

recognize you?"

"She did, but sort of kept fading in and out. She asked me when the game started, so maybe she thought we were going to see the Dodgers."

"I know exactly what you mean. She mixes up time with me quite a bit as well."

He shakes his head. "Geez, I can't get over how you look. It's like you just jumped right over all the years in between."

"Thanks. I'd love to say I had, but I lived through every one of them."

"I guess you're on your way in to see Ruth. She mentioned you a few times. It's good that you've stuck by her like you have. A lot of people might not have."

"Hey, you know Ruth. She's worth it."

"She sure is." He looks down and seems to be weighing something in his head. He clears his throat. "Say, listen, Victoria—" He hesitates and seems to lose his resolve. "Nah, forget about it."

"What is it?"

"Nah, I just ran into you after all this time. It wouldn't be right."

"Why don't you let me decide that?"

He silently debates it and purses his lips. "I hate to ask, but would you mind walking with me down to the corner? I'd like to pick your brain on something. I kind of need a lady's perspective."

Victoria looks at the door to the facility then gives Gino a wink. "Sure."

As they walk along, Gino says, "Say, remember that Dodgers game we went to?"

"I do. What ever happened to your friend, Jimmy?"

Gino shakes his head. "He never made it off Normandy beach."

"I'm sorry to hear that. He was a good guy. I know the two of you were great friends as well."

"We sure were. Hey, you remember that ball Jimmy caught, that he got signed by Dolph Camilli. When I got back from the war, his mother sent it to me."

"She did? I'd think she'd want to keep it, since it belonged to Jimmy."

"That's what I thought too, but she said that Jimmy made her promise that if anything happened to him, she'd give it to me."

"Do you still have it?"

"You know what I did? I took it up to Cooperstown and donated it to the Hall of Fame. I had them put on it that it was donated by James Falcone of Brooklyn. Anytime anyone walks in it's one of the first things they see. I took his Mom up to see it and she was real proud."

"That's nice. So, what was it you wanted to talk to me about?"

He looks down then away from her. "My son Franco and his wife died a few years ago and I've been looking after their kids, Bart and Theresa. They're good kids and I've tried to raise 'em right." He stops. "Theresa's in high school now and she's doing real good but — she's got herself into a situation. I mean, she's a good kid, but she was seeing this guy and—"

Victoria touches his arm. "I think I understand. Does she know what she wants to do about it?"

"That's the thing. See her and Bart, I raised them in the Church, and she knows what they have to say about it. But I want her to do what's right for her, you know? I don't want her doing what she thinks I want her to do, but I don't really know how to help her. My day, we didn't really talk about these kinds of things, but now—"

Victoria takes out one of her business cards then writes something on the back.

"Caring Hands has a center in Brooklyn, and they provide counseling for this type of situation." She hands him the card but flips it over first. "On back I've written the name of one of our best counselors. She'll listen and won't try to push Theresa into anything. She'll just put it all out there and let Theresa decide. Give her a call, tell her I referred you. I'm sure she can help Theresa decide what's right for her."

Gino takes the card and looks it over. "Candace Delaney. I'll have Theresa call her and I can take her over. I want to be there for her, but it should be her decision, you know?"

Victoria pats him on the shoulder. "It sounds like she's already in excellent hands. Good luck."

Theresa Morelli sits on her bed holding a pillow against her stomach and staring at the shelf where she displays the trophies she's won. She's average height and has a compact frame with dark curly hair and an olive complexion that tans easily. A distance runner, she's been on the varsity squad since, as a freshman, she beat the times of several senior athletes during tryouts. Since then, she's helped the squad come in first or second in every meet they've attended except for their most recent competitions which she's had to miss due to illness. She's also noticeably put on weight, but so far, no one at school seems to have put all the pieces together and Theresa has covered by saying that the weight is due to her not training as much as previously.

In fact, she knows what the true cause is and has known since a little more than a month after she and her boyfriend Michael Reiner, a sprinter from a rival school, spent a couple of nights together during a week-long track meet out of state. She and Michael broke up a week or so later and several weeks after that, she missed her period. Concerned but not terribly worried, she hopped on a train and went to a drug store near Central Park where she purchased an e.p.t. pregnancy test. She wasn't happy with the results, which lead her to visit a free clinic in another part of Brooklyn which confirmed her suspicions.

Her grandfather, Gino, who's raised Theresa and her brother since her parents died five years prior, came in that night to find her in tears in her room. When she told him why, he left the room and paced the floor in the kitchen for a while before returning and giving her a big hug.

"Listen kid, you need to figure out what you want to do about this. And whatever you decide, I'll be there with you, okay?"

His support makes things a bit easier, but she still doesn't know what she'll do. She's waiting for him to

TALES OF TWO SISTERS

come back from an appointment so he can drive her to a counseling center he's heard about. Finally, she hears his key in the front door and a few minutes later, he sticks his head into her room.

"You ready, kid?"

In the car, her grandfather reassures her. "Now the person who told me about this place says they won't try to get you do to anything you don't want. They're just going to listen and explain all the options."

"Options. That's a nice way to put it."

"Hey now, don't talk like that. There are a few things you could do about this. These people here, they can help you make the right decision for you, okay?"

She nods but doesn't look at him. He pulls over and gently touches her shoulder. "Listen kid. I want you to think about you right now, okay? I know you've been to church, and you know what they say, but when you go in there, you don't think about me or anything else, you just think about what's best for you, you hear? Whatever you decide, I'm still here for you and still love you."

Theresa looks at him with tears in her eyes and hugs him. "I love you Grandpa."

At the Caring Hands facility, Candace Delaney greets Gino and Theresa and invites them into her office. Gino rubs Theresa's back. "I think she'd like to talk to you alone."

"Are you sure?" Candace says to Theresa.

"Yes. It's my decision, so, yes."

Gino pats her back and winks at her. "I'll be right here waiting for you, kid."

In her office, Candace gets some information from Theresa. "How far along are you?"

"A little over two months," Theresa says to which Candace nods.

Candace removes some materials from her desk. "Now, I'm going to outline the various options you have and give you the pros and cons of each. Please understand I'm not endorsing any one of them, just letting you know what's there for you."

She hands Theresa a brochure outlining the pros and

178

cons of keeping the child.

"A child is a very big responsibility, but you obviously know that, otherwise you wouldn't be here. If you go this route, you'll definitely have to sacrifice a lot. On the other hand, it looks like you have good family support and that's always a plus. I'd strongly advise you to take parenting classes which could help you prepare. Is the father of the child in the picture?"

"No. I told him, but he doesn't want to have anything to do with it."

Candace nods and switches brochures. "You'll need to get that in writing if you decide to put the child up for adoption. The good news is, newborn children are the most desirable for people wanting to adopt, so there shouldn't be a problem placing him or her with a good family. However, you and the father will be required to give up all rights to the child. You won't be able to check in every week to see how he or she is doing."

"What if the kid wants to know who I am? Or maybe I want to see how the kid turns out as an adult?"

"There are ways to go about that if all parties agree, but you shouldn't count on that happening. In most cases, once the child is placed neither the child nor the parent sees one another again. But, if all parties agree, you may have a chance to meet with the adoptive parents and get a feel for the family the child will be raised in."

Theresa nods. "What about the last option?"

Candace gives her a pamphlet on abortion.

"It is a medical procedure and there are risks involved, but since legalization nine years ago, it has become commonplace and been made as safe as possible provided you go to a reputable clinic. We would refer you to a provider where you'll receive the best care and counseling." Candace sets her brochure down. "Now I do need to mention that most facilities prefer to perform the procedure during the first trimester. That would give you about two weeks. It can be done later, but many places do that only when there are complications. But, like I say, you still have a little time if this is how you want to proceed."

"Do a lot of girls choose this?"

"A fair number. Of course, we only know about the women we deal with, but other services probably have similar statistics."

Theresa looks over the materials she's been given. Candace smiles and says, "You don't have to make a decision right now and I'll be happy to answer any questions you have."

"If I decide to give the baby up for adoption, do you handle that?"

"No. We only do counseling, but we work with several excellent agencies that screen their applicants thoroughly, so you can be sure the child will be placed in a loving and caring home."

Theresa sits for several minutes going over each option. "That's that I want to do. Let someone adopt the baby."

"You don't need to decide right now. We generally recommend that women consider any decision for at least twenty-four hours."

"I'm not going to feel any different tomorrow or the next day. I can't take care of a kid and I don't want to have an abortion."

Candace nods. "Okay. We'll put you in touch with an agency, and in the meantime, if you have questions or second thoughts, you can call me." She hands Theresa a card. "That has all my numbers on it. Use any of them anytime if you need to talk."

As her visits with Ruth become more stressful, Victoria decides she needs some sort of release. She takes a walk around the area to see what's there and a few blocks from the nursing home, she finds a gym. The sign outside says, "Sign up for swimming lessons inside." Victoria has always wanted to learn to swim, so she goes in and signs up. Her first lesson is on Wednesday at four o'clock.

Victoria changes into a one-piece swimsuit and puts a towel around her neck, gripping it to conceal the scar as she goes to the check-in desk.

"Victoria Wells. I have a lesson at four-o-clock."

The attendant checks the schedule.

"Yes, Ms. Wells, you'll be working with Dana." He looks into the pool area. "She's currently in section two wearing a light blue suit."

Victoria heads toward section two and spots the woman in the light blue suit working with a child toward the shallow end of the pool. She pauses a moment to watch as the woman supports a little boy who's floating on his back. She slowly moves her hands away and says something to the child who smiles. Victoria continues to where they are. As she approaches, the woman turns to look at her and says something. Victoria freezes when she sees the woman's face. "Gisele?"

The woman gives her a curious look. "Miss?"

Victoria pulls herself together. "I'm sorry?"

"I said are you my four-o'clock?" *It's not Gisele's voice.*

"Yes, I am. Victoria. You must be Dana."

"Hi Victoria. I'll be finished here in a few minutes."

Victoria sits on a bench, trying to reconcile the image in the water in front of her with her memory from long ago. By the time Dana concludes the lesson, Victoria has discerned several differences between Dana and Gisele. Dana's legs and upper body are well developed but lack the lean definition of Gisele's. Dana jostles the hair of the little boy she had in the pool with her then turns and strides toward Victoria. Her gait is confident but not forceful. Gisele seemed to glide across the floor. "Ready to get started Victoria?"

"Yes."

"You can just drop your towel there." Dana waves toward the hooks along the wall. Victoria hesitates then hangs the towel up and follows Dana into the pool.

"Wow!" Dana says when she sees Victoria's neck. "Sorry, you probably don't like people bringing it up."

"It's kind of hard to miss."

"Well, I won't ask what happened, but if you want to volunteer the information—"

She gives a toothy smile. *Her teeth are better than Gisele's.*

"Maybe later."

Dana has Victoria float on her back, just as she had the

boy do earlier. Victoria lies back and floats atop the water, and for the first time in a long time she allows all the stress she's been under to drift away. They work on a few other moves and in what seems like no time at all, the lesson is over.

"Thanks, Dana, it was fun."

"Great. You're back tomorrow?"

"Yes. Same time."

"I'll see you then."

Dana turns to go.

"You wouldn't happen to dance would you?"

Dana turns and crosses her arms and raises an eyebrow.

"Are you asking me out to dance?"

Victoria blushes then considers it. "What if I was?"

Dana leans over to pat Victoria's shoulder. "I'd say maybe we should stick to the swimming for now."

Victoria nods without meeting Dana's eyes.

Dana starts to walk away but pauses and turns back.

"Ask me in a couple of weeks."

Theresa sits with Gino in a conference room at the adoption agency suggested to her by Caring Hands. She's now four months into her pregnancy and has, so far, managed to keep it a secret from her classmates. She's hoping she can make it into summer vacation before her condition becomes too obvious. While she's waiting, she entertains herself by occasionally spinning around in the swivel chair she's in.

"You nervous, Kid?"

"A little. What do you think they'll be like?"

"I don't know. The agency says they're top notch, though."

"Did they say if they're from New York?"

Gino looks up and away from her while he mulls this over. "I don't think they said."

Ten or fifteen minutes after her arrival, the agent returns, followed by a couple who appear to be in their early thirties. The man has broad shoulders and the earliest stages of a paunch around his waist. His dark hair is combed straight back. The woman is taller than the man, with a lively expression, light brown hair, and wearing glasses. The Morellis stand when they enter.

"Theresa and Gino, this is Byron and Marianne Eastbrooke."

Byron offers his hand and Gino leans across the table to shake it. Marianne takes Theresa's outstretched hand and cups it in hers. "We are so happy to meet you."

Almost immediately Theresa feels comfortable around them.

As she sits, Theresa says, "I got Mike — I mean — the father to sign the paperwork, so there's not going to be a problem there."

The Eastbrookes nod.

"We're very excited about having a new baby," Marianne says. "We have a little boy already, so the new child would have an older brother."

"Why do you want to adopt, if you don't mind my asking?"

Marianne looks down. "After our son George was born, I was diagnosed with uterine cancer. They got it all, but had to perform a hysterectomy in the process, so I can't have more children."

Byron adds, "But we've always wanted more, so adoption is perfect for us."

Theresa nods. "Are you in New York?"

"No, Connecticut," Byron says.

"The information we received is that you're an athlete," Marianne says. "What sport?"

"I run track," she says. "At least I did. Probably will again next year."

Byron and Marianne look at one another and nod. Byron says, "Maybe the child will inherit some of your abilities."

They speak for nearly an hour and in the end, Theresa decides that the Eastbrookes would be a good family for her child. They spend the remainder of the time discussing next steps.

Allison walks along the narrow hallway of an old office building in Bishopsgate looking for suite 109. She finds the door with the words "Daniel Seely, General Accountancy" on it. Just below this, in smaller print are the words, "Seely Family Association, London Division." She enters and presents herself to the receptionist.

"Allison Stepney here to see Mr. Seely."

"Ah yes. He's very anxious to speak to you and said to send you right in."

Allison enters the indicated office and is met by a tall, stocky, clean-shaven man with salt and pepper hair and a receding hairline, wearing a light-colored suit that's at least ten years out of style. He's reviewing a file, but when he sees Allison, he closes it and sets it on his desk then moves toward her with his hand extended. "Miss Stepney?"

"Yes, and you must be Mr. Seely."

He shows her to a chair then takes a seat behind his desk. He folds his hands on top of the desk. "I was delighted to hear from you. It's not every day I get to entertain a famous designer."

"You're very kind, but please, think of me as just another person with an interest in your family."

"Yes, yes. Your question was very intriguing. May I ask what sparked your interest in Victoria?"

Allison gives him the cover story she devised the evening before. "I was named after an earlier Allison Stepney and while I was researching her I ran across mention of a Vickie Seely who was somehow connected to her. Further research pointed me in your direction."

"I think I can provide you with some insight into the situation you're referencing, but I must admit, Victoria is a rather problematic figure among Seely researchers."

"Why do you say that?"

He thinks a moment then puts his arms on the desk and leans forward.

"My great-grandfather was Donald Seely. Victoria was his aunt, but there are almost no stories of her that have been handed down. His brother Willem has said that they didn't know any of their aunts and while they occasionally heard their aunt Amanda mentioned, Victoria's name was rarely spoken in the house and that was usually by their father when their mother wasn't around." He opens the file he was reading and removes a sheet of paper, which he hands across the desk to Allison. "This is a photocopy of a page from the family bible their parents maintained. Look at the listing for Thomas Seely."

Allison examines the page. The entries are all written in a careful, clear hand. Her eyes focus on the entry for "Thomas Seely m. Margaret Smythe" with the date. Underneath, in the same clear hand is the name "William Seely" with his birth date and the notation of his marriage. Below that, first is written "No bros/sis" in the same clear hand which is then marked through and underneath, on separate lines and written in a very rough and shaky hand "Victoria b. 1838 - unknown" then "Amanda b. 1840 - sent to Australia" then "Sarah b. 1848 - probably dead." Allison notes that Thomas' death date is a few years before Victoria was born.

Daniel says, "Willem has confirmed that the neat handwriting is his mother's, and the rougher hand is his father's. Most likely this change was made after his mother died."

"Sarah, 1848," Allison says to herself. To Daniel she says, "What should we make of this?"

"Good question." Daniel takes the sheet back from Allison. "Although I can say that the one thing that was handed down about Victoria was that she had a rather unsavory reputation. Unfortunately, my great-grandfather died in an accident on the docks around 1908. My grandfather was his youngest child and wasn't very old at the time, so very little of the family's history was passed down through him."

"That's too bad."

"But, Willem lived well into his nineties and was a veritable font of information on the family. I had the opportunity to speak with him on several occasions and it filled in a number of blanks in my research."

Daniel stops and considers something. "Do I—" he begins then stops as he looks in his middle drawer then removes a photo album from it. "Yes, here they are. I almost forgot that I have some photos of Donald and Willem."

"Do you?"

Daniel opens the album to a page and hands it to Allison. "My understanding is that these were taken on the occasion of their father's funeral."

"Rather odd event to commemorate in photos."

Daniel acknowledges this with a chuckle. "I believe it was one of the last times the family would be together. Willem and his family moved to Yorkshire a short time later."

Allison nods. She examines first the photo of both brothers with their wives and families. Something about one of the men seems vaguely familiar to her, but she can't say what. She flips the page to a larger photo featuring just the brothers. Allison's eyes go immediately to the suit one of the brothers is wearing. She holds up the photo. "Who's who in this photo?"

Daniel leans forward and squints. "Donald is on the right."

"You wouldn't happen to have a magnifying glass would you?"

Daniel pauses, his finger on his chin then, shakes his finger. "Yes, I believe so."

He goes to a cabinet near the desk and looks through it. "Ah!"

He brings her the glass and resumes his seat behind the desk. "May I ask what it is you see?"

"I'm not sure." Allison closely examines the suit Willem is wearing. To herself she says, "Jeffery's work."

She looks back to Mr. Seely. "I was hoping I could discern some details on the suit Willem is wearing. It looks remarkably similar to what Stepney & Sons was doing around this time period."

"You can tell that just by looking at a photo?"

"I'd be more certain if I could see the actual garment, the stitching. I suppose that's long gone."

"I would imagine. Willem died several years ago, and I believe the family donated most of his wearable clothes. Plus, a lot of his clothing was destroyed in a house fire while the family was away on holiday some years ago."

Allison closes and hands him the album. "Thank you so much for sharing these with me."

He puts the album in his middle drawer then rises and comes from behind the desk with some files and sits beside Allison. "As you've probably discerned, I head up the section of the family association devoted to Donald's descendants. My counterpart for Willem's descendants is Mrs. Agnes Robeson. After hearing from you, I spent an afternoon with Mrs. Robeson, and she reminded me of quite an interesting story I first heard from Willem. It seems that around 1902 both families came into quite a bit of money."

"Did they?"

"Yes, and the story both were given is that it was from their aunt Victoria. They were each told that she had gone to America, made something of herself and remembered them in her will."

"Awfully nice of her."

"It was, but there's a bit of a problem with that story. I've checked the records of passenger ships leaving England from 1850 through 1920 and have only found one listing for a Victoria Seely and that was in 1902."

"Could that have been her?"

"It doesn't seem probable. This woman listed her age as twenty-two and occupation as a musician. And there's more to it than that."

He thumbs through his file and removes several pages. "These are copies of police records from 1825 through 1900. There are dozens of mentions of a Vickie who's either wanted or has been arrested for a variety of offenses including robbery, assault, nuisance, and solicitation. She's even listed as a person of interest in a murder investigation."

"Was she a pickpocket?"

Daniel gives her a questioning look. "Why yes. How did you know that?"

Allison gives him a smile. "As I say, my namesake was associated with her. The association was that she was sometimes mistaken for her."

"Ah yes. I believe I have information on that." He looks through the file then removes a sheet. "A gentleman named Cedric Stepney filed numerous complaints with the police due to his daughter being mistaken for Vickie. He went so far as to take out an injunction against the police force."

"He certainly did." Allison fondly reminisces on the case then catches herself. "I mean that's what my research has shown."

Daniel thumbs through the file. "There's mention of Vickie in police records until November of 1888 then one final mention, where she was picked up for assault, but released without charges after a—" He breaks off and looks closely at the page. "Ah, it says a Mr. Bergeron took responsibility for her."

"Bergeron. Does it say how they were connected?"

"No, just that he vouched for her, and she was released. It's after this point that all public records of Victoria Seely stop. No police records, no parish records, no directory listings."

Allison leans forward. "Interesting."

"Admittedly, women are notoriously hard to track in public records since men had most of the rights, privileges, and authority, but I can find no evidence she married, had children, or died."

"Could this have been when she went to America?"

"Possibly, though I can find no evidence she did. Again, the only person by that name I can find is the one in 1902, when Victoria would have been sixty-four. I find it very hard to believe that a woman that age could fool anyone into believing she's just twenty-two."

"You'd be surprised." Daniel gives her an odd look. "What people will believe, that is."

"I suppose. But, as it turns out, there's yet another twist to the story."

He looks through another of his files. "These are clippings from various newspapers of the time." He hands the file to Allison. "Pay attention to the listings of performers in the music halls."

She scans through the listings, until she comes to "Mrs.

Carlotta Fox" in dark letters and below that, "Accompanied by Miss V. Seely." She looks through several other listings and everywhere Mrs. Fox shows up her accompanist is always V. Seely. V. Seely also shows up as the accompanist for several other singers and as a solo performer on one or two occasions.

"And you think this is Vickie?"

"I'm certain of it. Look at the bottom two pages."

Allison complies. The first is a listing in a London paper from 1899 for music lessons offered by "Miss V. Seely" and showing her address. The last page is a directory listing for "R. Bergeron" around 1900 and the address is the same one used by Miss Seely in the ad as well as on the card Allison has.

Allison shakes her head as she closes the file. "Could this be the same person throughout?"

"As I say, Vickie's history is rather problematic."

Allison hands him the file and he consults it as he speaks.

"Here's what the record shows: The police listings are very clear that it's the same Vickie from the late-1850s through 1888. We have a report of her sister Amanda being transported to Australia in 1861 for refusing to give evidence against her, but the record is clear on that. Vickie Seely shows up in police records until she becomes associated with Mr. Bergeron and after that we have no official documents on her as Vickie or Victoria. She simply vanishes. However, we later find V. Seely listed as an accompanist for various performers during the 1890s and offering music lessons from Mr. Bergeron's residence toward the turn of the century. Finally, in 1902, a Victoria Seely, who claims to be twenty-two years old and a musician left England for America. That same year, my great-grandfather and his brother received a substantial sum of money from their aunt Victoria who, it is claimed, went to America." He closes the file and leans back. "I find it very difficult to believe it's the same person, but if it isn't, I can't find much of a break between them. I can say this, though. If Victoria in 1902 is the same person as Vickie in the 1850s, she must have looked unnaturally young for her age."

Allison looks away then crosses her legs. "What became of Mr. Bergeron?"

Daniel swivels in his chair and leans his elbow on one of the arms. "He's another mystery. On the off-chance Victoria married him I attempted to trace her via his records. He's even more enigmatic, though I did find one interesting tidbit."

"What was that?"

"In 1902, a short while after Victoria Seely left for America, records show that R. Bergeron put his house and all its furnishings up for sale. The transaction was handled by Mr. Bergeron's solicitor as he had apparently left the country by that time. It's definitely the same address used by V. Seely in her ad for piano students."

"America?"

"It doesn't specify, but the note containing Mr. Bergeron's instructions was posted from Geneva according to the records."

Allison shakes her head. "It does seem very perplexing." A thought suddenly occurs to her. "What is Victoria's relationship to you?"

Daniel gives her a wide grin. "Alive or dead, Vickie would be my great-great-grand-aunt."

Allison lays her hand on his. "Mr. Seely, I very much appreciate your taking the time to speak to me. This is all very fascinating, learning about this person who may have had a connection to someone close to me."

"The pleasure is all mine, and please, if you ever run across any evidence to make some sense of all this, do be sure to send a copy."

"I certainly will." She stands. "I'm afraid I must be going, but please, let's keep in touch."

"I would be delighted. Perhaps we can compare notes again."

"Perhaps."

Outside on the street, Allison looks skyward. "Ah, Victoria. If only we'd met back then. How our lives might have changed."

She makes a mental note to try to learn more about

the woman Harry saw in New York, but once she returns to the hustle and bustle of the business, particularly after Peter makes good on his pledge to retire to Florida to spend the rest of his life fishing with Harry, the idea gets pushed further and further back until she hardly thinks of it at all. Every year around Christmas she gets a card from Daniel but never makes a return trip to his office.

Dana and Victoria have been out on another of their "just friends" dates. Even though both are strongly attracted to one another, Victoria has insisted on not allowing the relationship to go much further due to a mysterious "situation" Victoria's in but refuses to discuss.

"It's not about trust. I trust you, Sweetie, but I also know how complicated my situation is. The only reason I can make sense out of it is that I'm in the middle of it. Otherwise, it's incomprehensible."

So, they continue meeting one another every few days, sometimes grabbing a bite to eat, maybe watching a movie but almost never spending any time alone. Tonight is an exception. Victoria seems more stressed out than usual, so Dana has proposed a walk along the promenade in Brooklyn.

After nearly an hour of strolling and making small talk, they find a bench and sit, Victoria staring out at the water without speaking and Dana looking at her with concern. Dana lays her hand on Victoria's and Victoria looks over, meeting Dana's eyes. Dana tentatively leans in and kisses Victoria lightly on the lips. Then Victoria returns it, and they kiss for several seconds. Victoria looks at Dana then turns away, tears in her eyes.

"No."

"What's wrong?"

Victoria does not turn to face her. "It would be very easy to fall in love with you."

"Why don't you?"

Victoria shoots a quick glance at her.

"I already have, but my life is too complicated right now. There's someone who needs me to be there."

"Is this the person in the nursing home?"

"How did you—"

Dana chuckles. "I swear I wasn't spying on you. I saw you going in there the other day while I was walking to work. I waved but I guess you didn't see me."

"She's a big part of it."

"Vickie, listen, I want to help you. I want to be there for you. Just tell me what you need."

Victoria touches Dana's face and kisses her.

"What I really need right now is a friend."

"I'll be whatever you need me to be." Dana gives Victoria a quick hug and they sit silently until Victoria's cell phone rings.

"Hello? That's me. Yes." She closes her eyes and is silent for a moment. "When did it happen? Did she— Oh, she was asleep. Yes, her arrangements are on file. I'll be by later for her things. Thank you, you're very kind."

She hangs up.

"Vickie?"

Victoria stares ahead, her lower lip quivering, her breathing quickening. Absent-mindedly, to herself she says, "It's over, dearest. It's over."

She covers her eyes and leans forward, breaking into heavy sobs. Dana puts her arms around Victoria and leans her head against Victoria's.

"I'm here, Vickie. I'm here."

On August 18, 1982, at 8 p.m., Theresa Morelli is admitted to the maternity ward of Brooklyn Hospital. Two hours later, she delivers a healthy six-pound four-ounce baby girl. The hospital keeps them overnight for observation, but the next morning, Theresa is told she is ready to be released. Gino and the Eastbrookes are there, and the nurse brings in the baby. Theresa notices her nametag.

"Eleanor Rigby. Like the song."

The nurse chuckles. "I'd like to think McCartney wrote it for me, but my parents weren't really into The Beatles."

Nurse Rigby gives the baby to Theresa, and steps aside. Theresa holds the baby for a few minutes then kisses her on the forehead.

"You be a good kid okay?" Tears are streaming from her eyes. "These are your parents now. They'll take good care of you. Have a great life, kid."

She hands the baby to Marianne.

"We will take very good care of her," Marianne says.

"Do you know what you're going to name her?"

Byron and Marianne look at one another and Byron says, "We've decided on Dana. That's Marianne's mother's name."

Theresa nods. "That's a good name."

"We don't know about a middle name, though." Marianne gives Theresa a slight smile.

A name pops into Theresa's head. "What about Bethany?"

"Bethany?" Marianne says.

"That was my mother's name. She died a few years ago with my dad."

"Dana Bethany," Marianne says. "I like that."

Marianne gives Dana to Byron and hugs Theresa. "Thank you so much for bringing this joy into our lives. I promise you we will take good care of her for as long as we live."

Victoria and Dana enter Victoria's apartment. She spreads her arms. "Mi casa."

"This is a great place. Why didn't you want to bring me here?"

"There's stuff here that's hard to explain."

Dana strolls around looking at the paintings and framed pictures on the credenza below the art wall.

"You play the piano?" Dana runs her hand along the baby grand in the corner.

"I do. A few other instruments, too."

Dana focuses on a framed photo, hanging away from the others on the wall and steps over to it. It's a very old photo of a dancer, blond and very athletic. She's posing in fourth position, which emphasizes the muscle definition in her legs and arms. Dana is stuck by how graceful she looks. She turns to Victoria to ask her something and finds Victoria staring at her, one arm across her body, the other leaning on it with her fist covering her mouth.

"Is something wrong?"

"It's just — the picture, it's—"

"She's beautiful." Dana looks back at the photo. "Who is she?"

"Her name's Gisele Bourgeois. She was a dancer in Paris in the late 1800s."

As she examines the photo, it suddenly occurs to Dana that she bears a strong resemblance to the dancer. "Why do you have this here?"

"She's very special to me." Victoria doesn't look at Dana.

"Someone who was probably long gone before you were even born. How is she special? Are you related?"

Victoria turns away and covers her eyes.

"This is why I've been hesitant to bring you up here. So many questions and I'm not sure I can give you answers you're going to believe."

"Damn it, Vickie." Dana throws her hands up and approaches Victoria. "You say you love me then you give me these cryptic answers to the simplest questions."

"There are no simple questions where I'm concerned, and the answers are even more complex."

"Vickie, you know you can tell me anything. I'll understand."

"You'll understand anything?" Victoria walks to Gisele's picture. "What if I told you that Gisele is special to me because I knew her, loved her. She was my first true love, after I found out some interesting things about myself." She touches the glass as a tear runs down her cheek. "We met in Paris and spent four years together on and off. Then she got sick and when I found out I went to take care of her. She died in my arms." Tears are now flowing from her eyes, and she wipes her cheeks with the sleeve of her shirt.

"What are you telling me, Vickie? How could you possibly have known her? You'd have to be—"

Victoria looks Dana squarely in the eye. "One hundred

and sixty-six years old."

Dana gives her a disbelieving stare, trying to process what she's been told.

"The woman who was in the nursing home — I was in love with her as well. We met in the thirties and were together sixty-four years."

Victoria moves to the center of the living room and spreads her arms, turning one way then the other.

"I didn't inherit this place from my aunt. I bought it in 1922. I've been living here since."

"Vickie, this is crazy. I just wanted you to be honest with me for once."

"I'm being honest with you! I don't age the same as an average person. I age a lot slower—"

Dana throws her hands up and heads for the door.

"Okay that's it. I'm not staying here if you're just going to play games with me."

Victoria blocks her way and grabs her arms.

"Dana, please. This is the reason I didn't tell you sooner because I knew you'd react like this." She motions toward the couch. "Please, sit down. I have some things to show you. Once you've seen them, if you still want to go, I won't stop you." Dana won't look at her. "Just give me half an hour. Please."

Dana sighs. "I guess I owe you that much."

She sits on the couch.

Victoria disappears into the bedroom and reappears carrying several scrapbooks and photo albums. She lays them on the coffee table.

"The strange history of Victoria Wells. Look through these and then I'll answer any questions you ask, no matter how painful." She picks up one and hands it to Dana. "Start with this one."

She disappears into the bedroom again. Dana opens the scrapbook and the first thing her eyes fall on is immigration papers for "Miss Victoria Wells, age 22, London, England 29 October 1902." Beside the immigration papers is a very old photo of a woman who looks like Victoria posing with an older woman. Below the image of the older woman is written "Elizabeth Mayfair."

She flips through the pages to a piece of sheet music entitled "Starlight and Memories" authored by "V. Wells." The copyright date is 1904. On the next page she finds another photo of the woman who resembles Victoria, only this time she's dressed in men's clothing and holding a hat. Beside it is another shot of her wearing the hat and posing with four Black men who are holding instruments. The Victoria look-a-like is seated at a piano. In another one, she's standing with a lone Black man in the same setting as the group shot and below this one is written "Scott Joplin." There are also several photos of the woman with an attractive Black woman who appears to be a little older. In some she's dressed as a man, in others she's wearing dresses in the style of the early 20th century.

Dana sets the scrapbook aside then opens one of the photo albums and gasps. It's another picture of the Victoria look-a-like shot from the waist up, but now she's wearing a low-cut dress in the style of the late-nineteenth century. Though she's wearing a necklace, Dana can clearly see the scar on her neck.

"Vickie?"

She spends another hour going through the photos and in some, she can also see the scar.

Finally, she closes the last of the scrapbooks and heads into the adjacent room. Victoria is seated in an overstuffed chair near the window, her knees pulled up tight against her chest, her arms around her legs and her head resting on her knees.

"You're still here. That's a good sign."

"As crazy as this all sounds, I believe you. But I have to ask you a question and I need you to be totally honest with me."

"Anything, sweetie."

"Are you with me because I remind you of her?" She points toward the photo of Gisele.

Victoria closes her eyes. "When I first saw your face, it knocked the wind out of me. It was like I was looking at her again."

She pulls herself out of the chair and goes to Dana,

taking her hands and looking deep into her eyes. "But, sweetie, you're nothing like Gisele. Yes, you're both blond and athletic and your face has similar features, but that's where the resemblance ends." She touches Dana's cheek. "You don't talk like her, you don't act like her, and you certainly don't dance like her."

"I can dance."

"The way you carry yourself. The way you feel when I hold you is completely different. Believe me, I was familiar with every inch of her body—" Dana raises an eyebrow. "Sorry." She turns away and walks back toward the chair. "The more I get to know you, the similarities become less and less. I see you, not her."

She walks back and sits on the bed. "I loved Gisele. I loved her with all my heart and when she died, I lost a part of myself. With Ruth, I knew it was coming for a long time, but Gisele was so young, and her death was so sudden I wasn't ready to deal with it. I've never been able to fill the void her death left inside me, and I suspect I never will. But to believe I could recreate her through you? That's not fair to you and it's not fair to her memory. When I look at you, all I see is an exceptionally beautiful and unique person with whom I am totally in love. When we turn out the lights, it's you and not her I feel next to me, and I wouldn't want that any other way."

Dana is crying and Victoria stands up and wipes the tears away then kisses Dana on each cheek. "Does that answer your question?"

She's unable to speak and instead nods. Victoria wraps her arms around Dana and holds her close. "You've got nothing to worry about, Sweetie. I'm yours, totally."

REUNITED

It is the first day of August 1997, and the sun has only been out for an hour when Victoria arrives at a small cemetery in Perth, Australia.

The driver hops out to open the door for her. "Hope your visit is enjoyable, ma'am."

"I'm sure it will be."

She pays him and thanks him for being a knowledgeable and interesting tour guide then asks him not to wait.

He hands her his card. "While you're here, should you be in need of reliable transportation, don't hesitate to call on Roland Renard."

"Sure thing, Roland. Take care."

Victoria makes her way across the grounds, stopping before the graves of Jonathan and Amanda Baynes. Amanda's life dates are 1840-1925. Victoria lays a single rose on Amanda's grave then sits on the small bench nearby.

"I finally found you, Mandy. Sorry I couldn't come any sooner." She wipes away a tear. "I hear you married a good man and raised five kids. You had a nice long life. If you don't mind, I'll sit with you for a while."

She folds her hands in her lap and sits with her head down, weeping silently.

As she sits there, an old woman using a cane crosses the grounds. Spotting Victoria, she alters her course and approaches Victoria from behind. She stops beside the bench.

"Excuse me, Miss. Are you here to pay your respects to the Baynes family?"

Victoria looks up then wipes her face. "Amanda, actually. I'm a relative."

"You don't say. I'm Jane Fuller. Amanda's my grandmother."

"Was she? Amanda had a sister, Victoria." She tries to count the right number of generations in her head. "I'm her, um, descendant. Victoria Wells."

Jane sits beside Victoria and pats her on the knee.

"Glad to see the name has remained in the family. I've actually heard quite a bit about your Vickie."

"You have?"

"When I was a little girl, my grandmother used to tell me all about her life in England and the family she left behind. She really loved her sister."

"I can tell you with absolute certainty that her sister loved her."

"If you've got time, why don't you come home with me? I'm the family historian and have quite a few letters and pictures."

"I'd like that."

At Jane's house, Victoria sits at a table in the dining room as Jane retrieves several archival boxes from a shelf in the corner. She sets the last of the boxes on the table and sits, then opens a photo album, and hands it to Victoria.

"This is Amanda on her wedding day."

Victoria takes it and looks again at the face of her sister several years older than Victoria remembers her, standing beside a thin man with light colored hair and a wide smile. Amanda is holding a bouquet and wearing a veil pulled back away from her face. She looks very happy.

I always thought I'd be there on your wedding day, Mandy, Victoria thinks as tears start to roll down her cheeks. *You made a beautiful bride.*

Jane is looking at her strangely.

"Victoria, may I ask you something? When I first found you at the grave, it seemed you were awfully broken up. Now you're crying over the photo of someone you've never even met. I'm just wondering why."

Victoria looks over at her and wipes her cheek and sets the album on the table.

"Jane, I'm afraid I wasn't entirely honest with you. I'm not Victoria's descendant. See, I can't have children. You knew your grandmother, but so did I. I called her Mandy. She's my sister."

"I don't understand. Surely you're not suggesting you're that Victoria."

"That's me." As she speaks, traces of her Cockney accent become more pronounced. "Did Mandy tell you about our brother Billy? He was our protector. I can't count the times he saved us while we were out wandering the streets of Wapping or Aldgate. He was the only one of the three of us who could write. All the letters we sent; he wrote 'em. Of course, he taught me how to scratch out a few words. Usually 'I love you too' only I spelled it l-u-v-e and y-u and t-o-e. I couldn't even spell my own name. I always wrote it V-I-K-E."

Jane removes one of the letters and looks at the bottom of the page where she finds the words written in a rough hand and spelled exactly as Victoria has mentioned.

"There's no way you could have known that. It's not the sort of information that gets passed down within families. But how can you be Vickie?"

Victoria laughs. "I wish I could explain. Why was it me and not Mandy? Not Billy?"

She hands the album back to Jane. "In a way, I'm responsible for you being here, Jane. I was the pickpocket. Mandy was never very good at it. She just didn't have the touch and was always getting caught. I tried to teach her, but only so much of it can be learned. I had a light touch." She holds up her right hand. "Small hands with long fingers. I could lift change out of someone's pocket, wallets, watches — I even took a pair of cufflinks off a guy once. But Mandy wanted so much to be like her big sister, she just kept trying and kept getting caught. I was the one the authorities wanted but she refused to tell them anything. She might never have been sent down if she had."

She shifts in the chair so she's facing Jane who's staring intently at her. "I still remember the last time I saw her. I'd run all over town that day trying to scrounge up cash. I hit up Billy and his co-workers, even people I barely knew. When I finally had enough, I ran down to the courthouse hoping I'd be in time to get her out of there, but I was too late. I held her until they pulled her away from me to put her on the wagon."

"She told me about that. She said Vickie did everything she could, but in the end, Grandma decided it was for the best."

"She was always the optimistic one. No matter what happened, she saw the good side of it. I did everything I could to shield her from the bad stuff."

"She knew that too. I never understood what she meant, but she once told me that she was sorry she never got around to thanking her sister for all Vickie did to protect her in the orphanage. It was the one regret she carried to her grave."

"I'd have done a lot more than that. I love her and not a day goes by that I don't miss her."

Jane pats Victoria's hand then looks in her boxes again. "Let me show you something."

She hands Victoria a photo of Amanda, who appears to be in her late forties. She and the thin man are standing with three boys and two girls of various ages in front of them.

"That's Jonathan, Amanda and their children." She points to the smallest daughter. "That's my mom Cassidy Rae."

She fishes out another photo which appears to be from the early part of the twentieth century. Now Amanda and Jonathan are much older and surrounded by a group of younger adults and several children.

"That's their children and grandchildren from 1918." Jane points out a small girl sitting in Amanda's lap. "And that's me."

She pulls out another photo, this one in color. "This is from our most recent Baynes's reunion."

The photo depicts a crowd of a hundred or more individuals of all ages gathered in a field in front of a small house.

She winks at Victoria. "And not everyone attended this one."

Jane hands Victoria one more photo of a girl eight to ten years old whose face almost mirrors that of Amanda when she was that age. "That's my great-granddaughter, Amanda Cassidy Davis."

Victoria smiles through the tears streaming down her cheeks.

Jane grasps Victoria's hand. "You see, Vickie. Your

Mandy's not dead. She lives on in all of us."

"Thank you, Jane." Victoria hands the photos back then wipes her eyes. "I'm so glad I met you."

"So am I, Vickie. Now I have quite a few questions for you."

They spend several hours together, looking at photos and letters and Victoria writing out what she remembers about Amanda and their family.

Around three-o-clock Jane's great-granddaughter, Mandy, comes by for a visit with her parents and siblings. In person, Mandy's resemblance to Victoria's Amanda is even more striking. Victoria has her picture taken with the family.

Jane opens the wedding album. "These are more shots from Amanda's wedding day."

The first few photos are of the bride and bridesmaids. Next is a shot of the entire wedding party and as Victoria looks over it, her eyes settle on a tall, broad-shouldered man standing beside Jonathan. His hair is very long, but something about his face looks familiar.

"Do you know who that is?" Victoria points to the man.

"Let's see if it's written on the back. No, it just says 'wedding party'." She flips the page and there's another shot of Jonathan with the broad-shouldered man. Jane looks on back. "It says, 'Baynes with Fox'."

"Fox — or Renard," Victoria says.

Jane looks at the photo again. "Now that you mention it, he does look a bit like Mr. Renard."

"You know Roland Renard?"

"Yes, but I can't for the life of me tell you how we met. He's just always been around. You don't suppose he's another one like you, do you?"

"Hard to say." She looks over the photos again. "It looks like they had a great time."

"Too bad you weren't able to make it."

The following morning, Victoria leaves her hotel and walks past the line of cabs until she catches sight of Roland Renard leaning against the door of his. She waves, and he jumps to attention, opening the door for her.

"Good morning, ma'am. Hope your previous trip was

fruitful."

"It was fun and very educational."

"Where can I take you today?"

"I've heard there are some places with phenomenal views of the ocean around here. Perhaps you could take me to one of those."

He considers it then snaps his fingers.

"I know just the place."

"And you might as well charge me the daily rate. I want to spend some time checking them out."

"Right-o."

When they get to the first observation spot, Victoria gets out and invites Roland to join her.

"Renard is the French equivalent of Fox, isn't it?"

"That's right."

She nods. "I should have remembered that, but even if I had, I'm not sure I'd have connected you to Charlie and Renee." When she says this he turns to stare at her. "Though you definitely have your mother's eyes."

Roland grins. "You know my parents?"

"I do. They're two of my oldest friends, but I haven't seen them in a long, long time."

"You're one of us!"

"I am, but right now I want to talk about someone who wasn't."

"Who's that?"

She stares out at the sea for a long moment.

"Tell me everything you can remember about Amanda Seely."

www.ingramcontent.com/pod-product-compliance
Lightning Source LLC
Chambersburg PA
CBHW031420250626
47155CB00004B/1561